HEMKHAM

A Theological Paradigm
for Reconciliation in the Kuki Society

HEMKHAM

A Theological Paradigm
for Reconciliation in the Kuki Society

Lunkholen Baite

2019

Hemkham: *A Theological Paradigm for Reconciliation in the Kuki Society* – published by the Rev. Dr. Ashish Amos of the Indian Society for Promoting Christian Knowledge (ISPCK), Post Box 1585, Kashmere Gate, Delhi-110006.

Online Order: http://ispck.org.in/book.php

ISBN: 978-93-88945-38-7

Cover design: Upa Jamsei Baite

Photography: Samuel Haokip

The house in the cover page is a traditional Kuki house made of thatch, woods, wild ropes and other materials bestowed by nature. The people standing in front of the house are adorned in Kuki traditional attires. The pole erected in front of the house is known as Sol-khom which is a symbol of success, affluence, power and dignity. Usually, it was erected in front of the house of Haosa (village Chief). However, others too were accorded the honor of erecting the pole in recognition of their act of valor, prosperity and other distinguished services they have rendered for the welfare of the community.

Laser typeset by

ISPCK, Post Box 1585, 1654, Madarsa Road, Kashmere Gate, Delhi-110006 • *Tel:* 23866323

e-mail: ashish@ispck.org.in • ella@ispck.org.in
website: www.ispck.org.in

Dedicated to my
Buddy, son and mentor

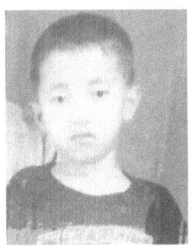

Master Nelson Thanggoukai @ Kakai Baite (2004-2012)
Who in the brevity of his life stood beside me
When my life was at its lowest ebb by
Anchoring me, trusting me and encouraging me
Leaving me for his Heavenly Home when
Convinced that he has made a servant of God
Out of his Dad

Contents

Acknowledgement

A s I look back at the different phases of this journey, undoubtedly, it was a series of sleepless, reflexive and confounding night and days. Now that it's over, I am happy to say that it was a journey filled to the brim with adventure and exploration. Indeed, I have to admit with all honesty that many have helped me in touching the "finishing line". Prof. Tlanghmingthanga, my thesis guide; gave me the zone to exercise my credibility free of interference, for this, I am indebted to him. At the same time, Rev. Laldingluia's insightful suggestions and comments helped the flow of my thoughts to find its own course- I owe him a lifelong. To the complete denial of themselves, my parents Mr. Hemkhothang Baite and Mrs. Lhingboi Baite have been my constant inspiration; with utmost love and care, they have made me 'the man' I am today. This achievement is the result of their selfless supports and prayers, and "I am proud to have them as my parents". Besides, my heart still throbs at the sacrifices made by my adorable wife Tinnu Baite, daughter (Choikim) and son (Gungou). They have during the entire period of the writing of this book wrestled with the brunt of my absence-their perseverance has made me undaunted. For this, I pledge with my life to love them all the more.

In fact, my research on *Hemkham* would have never begun without the consent of Eastern Manipur Presbytery and Manipur Presbyterian Church Synod. Their recommendation has fetched me the financial sponsorship from Mizoram Presbyterian Church Synod, without which my M.Th. course completion would still remain a "wistful wish". Besides, Litan Sareikhong Baptist Church and B. Phaicham Presbyterian Church had helped me out on several occasions. They have made my days during the research comfortable by their prompt responses whenever sought for; my thanks are due to them. There are many others whom I have not mentioned here. However, this doesn't in any way demean their contributions, truly, their "Samaritan acts" are well engraved in my heart.

This book in its original form was the thesis submitted to the Senate of Serampore College (University), towards M.Th. degree, which is published through written permission. Initially, the publication was impeded by financial problems; however, Th. Letkhotinthang Haokip, a brother and a friend came to my rescue at the nick of time; without him my entire two years effort would have remained forlorn. I am blessed to have him. Most of all, the timely consent of ISPCK to co-publish this book has been crucial in the successful publication of this book. Knowing that all these come from God alone spurs me to work more zealously for my Jesus. Without God's Providence this accomplishment would not have been made possible. Blessed be God's name.

Foreword

In keeping with the name of the book, *Hemkham: A Theological Paradigm for Reconciliation in the Kuki Society*, the author at once bombards you with the different facets of conflict deluging the Kuki society, in order to reiterate his stance on the need for Reconciliation in the Kuki Society and the world at large. And he never lets up on it. This succinctly written book is more than what it appears on the surface. Therefore, unless one gets down to a serious reading, the inherent truth would not come by quite easily. Besides, many would find it difficult to digest the necessity of the fusion of *Hemkham* and the Christian concept of Reconciliation which is the outcome of the life, death and resurrection of Jesus Christ. It would even be more difficult on the part of the intellectuals who are not trained theologically to imbibe the message of the book which the author painstakingly attempts to convey. The difficulty in grasping this fact is the surreptitiously continuing operation of the colonial mandate in the way we look, see, live and accept the truth as conditioned by the colonial past.

However, once the idea is grasped, this is where the beauty of the book lies; and this fact is what makes the book a must read. Perhaps, throwing the door open to the rich traditional heritage of the Kukis, especially, the practices associated with Conflict resolution in his maneuver to formulate a theology based on *Hemkham* is what makes the endevour of the author all the more worth noting. In the post colonial era, when almost everywhere; attempts have been made to untie the knots of the legacy of colonialism, it is sacrosanct not to attempt to relieve ourselves from the cultural homogenization process. And it is this attempt, on the part of the author, to rope in indigenous culture to revamp the gospel of Jesus Christ so that it becomes more relevant to the receivers which accords him appreciation. Along the course of the theological articulation, the author presents the Kukis to the world- who they are and what they stand for. The book is also a manual for those wishing to know the rich cultures, traditions and conflict resolution practices of the Kukis. It will surely help those involved in reconciliation ventures.

Hemkham hitherto considered as having nothing to do with the salvific and reconciling works of Jesus Christ has been given a new lease of life through the author's attempt to formulate a theology out of it. This book reveals the feasibility of employing Kuki traditions and cultures to propagate the Gospel of Jesus Christ more effectively and efficiently. On several occasions, in the face of life' severities, the Kuki tribal Christians fail to relate the realities overwhelming them with the truth of the Gospel. This is because, the cultures, belief system, practices and worldview with which the gospel has been wrapped are alien to them. Besides, the way the Gospel was passed on to them didn't recognize their culture, tradition, ethos and practices which had shaped and sustained them across the ages. On this line, the author by synthesizing tradition and gospel churns the relevancy of the Gospel afresh to the Kukis in particular and other people around the world. Every tribal feels certain yearning to retrieve the theological values of their trampled customs, cultures and practices, so that they can experience God in the way most relevant to their context. This book, in more ways than one, is an answered prayer to the long overdue yearning of the Kukis. I believe, this book is here to say that tribal cultures, traditions and practices are God given, and they are to be promoted rather than being shunned. Besides, it's my hope and prayer that this book will bring true reconciliation in the recalcitrant lives of the people around the world.

Rev. D.C. Haia
Moderator,
Council for World Mission (CWM)

Preface

The book, *Hemkham: A Theological Paradigm for Reconciliation in the Kuki Society* is a priority reading for anyone willing to explore the viability of fusing indigenous culture with the Christian faith. The fusion of the two is proposed so that it can be used as the basis for formulating a tribal theology based on *Hemkham*, in order to make the gospel more relevant to the Kukis and other indigenous people. At length, it dwells on parading the predicaments of the Kuki community and how the traditional practice of *Hemkham* with its reconciliatory dynamism continually helps them in sustaining their society in the midst of enmity, conflicts and bloodsheds. Perhaps the book is a manual for interacting with the history, traditions, cultures and traditional practices related to conflict resolution of the Kuki community. The Kuki society being deluged with conflict and its consequential bloodsheds requires a model for reconciliation is what the book is all about. At the same time, there is an underlying message of the urgency for reconciliation around the world for one and sundry running through out the book. Just when others have begun to believe that "all is not well with the Kuki society", hope is roped in through the attempt to synthesize the concept and the practice of *Hemkham* with the Christian concept of reconciliation. On this line, the fusion of the two is possible only if the reconciling dynamism present in the practice of *Hemkham* can be theologically authenticated. Thus, in order to synthesize *Hemkham* and Christian Reconciliation, the similarities and the differences between the two are laid out. Though not identical, *Hemkham* and the reconciliation wrought out through the life, death and resurrection of Christ are found to be similar on varying degrees. The similarities found, out of the comparison are used to authenticate the theological values of *Hemkham*. In the attempt to formulate a tribal theology out the fusion of Christian concept of reconciliation and the Kuki traditional practice of *Hemkham,* the theological values of the reconciling dynamism present in the performance of *Hemkham* which has been lying theologically unexplored have been retrieved. It is with utmost humility that the author embarks on this concerted venture to say that the Kuki cultures, traditions, customs and traditional practices of conflict resolution can be used to propagate the Gospel of Jesus Christ more relevantly to them and to other indigenous people as well. In fact, being the first book on this buried and forlorn topic, it is a lifetime encyclopedia on the realities, lives and struggles of the Kukis along with their rich traditions of conflict resolution. It is the hope of the author that immense profit will be developed through the reading of this context-relevancy quest book.

Rev. Lunkholen Baite

Introduction

In the age when estrangement, enmity, conflicts and killings have been ravaging the society so decisively, a theological paradigm for initiating reconciliation in the society is required. On this line, in order to surmount the conflicts and its consequent redundant killings in the Kuki society, a retrieval of the reconciliatory dynamism present in the Kuki traditional practice of *Hemkham* is imperative for the promotion of Peace and Reconciliation in the society. As such, this book focuses on the retrieval of the swaddled reconciliatory dynamism of *Hemkham* through the Christian's periscope, so that, it could be synthesized with the Christian reconciliation for formulating a theology based on *Hemkham*.

Traditionally, conflict resulting in bloodshed is reconciled by the performance of *Hemkham* in the Kuki society. However, with the advent of Christianity, some begin to consider *Hemkham* to be of the heathen's realm. Yet another group continues to hold it to be in line with the Christian's concept of reconciliation. Subsequently, these diverging views resulted in the polarization of *Hemkham* and Christian reconciliation. *Hemkham* being embedded in the Kuki cultural ethos has its dominance in the social and secular realm. On the other hand, Christian concept of reconciliation while having its significance in the spiritual aspect is doubted to resolve practical problems. As a result, this polarization impedes the fusion of the Christian understanding of reconciliation with that of the Kukis' traditional process of conflict resolution. As such, unearthing the theological values of the reconciling dynamism of *Hemkham* is inevitable to purge this polarization. This unearthing as a result will sanctify the theological authenticity of *Hemkham* and consolidates it for formulating a theology of reconciliation- a Kuki perspective based on *Hemkham*. Besides, the synthesized concepts of *Hemkham* and Christian reconciliation could be applied in the strife torn Manipur in particular and the world at large in general to address the rampant conflicts and its follow-on killings. In essence, the concept and practice of *Hemkham* involves an offering and killing of *Vohchal-Tuhnga*[1] by the culprit at the behest of the *Haosa*[2] as a penance for any premeditated or accidental killing/murder. It is performed to evade the use of weapons in retaliation so that reconciliation could be realized through the act of penance of the offering and killing of *Vohchal-tuhnga* and *Ankong-sokhom*[3] (a fellowship feast) which usually follows.

In fact, the description on *Hemkham* would be rather too vast if the Kukis as a whole are considered, because they live in different parts of Northeast India, Myanmar and Bangladesh and followed different Christian traditions with minor variations in the practice of their customary laws. Given this fact, the scope is delimited to the Kukis of Manipur as a field of reference because the largest Kuki concentration is found in Manipur state.

In order to build a foundational pedestal, the conflict situations in which the Kukis have been dragged into is laid out in the first chapter. The Kukis reel under the different ethnic conflicts: Anglo-Kuki, Kuki-Naga, Kuki-Meitei, Kuki-Zomi and inter-factional conflicts. Different memoranda and pacts have been signed between the Kukis and other communities in Manipur. Sadly, there is no desirable outcome and no official agreement has been signed yet between Kuki and Naga till today. Presently, the most serious problems the Kuki face is the factional clashes between the cognate tribes, factions and their disagreement with the Naga. Besides, there is the thorny issue of the majority Meiteis encroaching upon the hilly tribal areas of Manipur, most of which happen to be in Kuki-dominated area. Therefore, the call for reconciliation dominates the wish of every Kukis.

In Chapter two and three, the concepts and practice of reconciliation both from the Christian and traditional Kuki understanding respectively are examined. In the Christian understanding and concept, reconciliation between God and humans, and between humans was wrought out through Jesus Christ. The Kuki society being pigmented with conflicts, often witnesses its resultant killings. For that reason, *Hemkham* is usually performed to prevent retaliations and evade its consequent killings in the Kuki society. It is a traditional practice that brought two antagonistic person/groups together for reconciliation and plays a vital role in realizing reconciliation between persons, families, villages and clans.

Interestingly, even before the dawn of Christianity, *Hemkham's* role was vital in curbing the propensity toward killing one another and in dispensing peace and reconciliation in the society.

Finally, in chapter Four, both the Christian and *Hemkham* concepts of reconciliation are synthesized and employed to propose a formulation of contextual theology of reconciliation. Today, the need for theologizing from the Kuki perspective is realized and a few Kuki theologians started using the local resources in order to communicate the gospel message relevantly. On the same line, *Hemkham* is used herein as a source to develop a contextual theology of reconciliation, from the Kuki perspective. Thus, by fusing Christian understanding of reconciliation and the Kuki practice of reconciliation through *Hemkham*, *Ankong-sokhom* (a fellowship of feast) is proposed as a model for Kuki reconciliation.

Endnotes

[1] *Vohchal-tuhnga* refers to a boar measuring five palms breath, implying big enough for a feast.

[2] *Haosa* refers to Chief of a village (usually the eldest man of a clan genealogically).

[3] Literally, *Ankong* means plate and *sokhom* means sharing, *Ankong-sokhom* means the sharing of meal.

Chapter - 1

A Call for Reconciliation among the Kuki

The world we live in is pervaded with conflicts. Sadly, the advancement made in science and technology is exploited to increase the possession of weapons of mass destruction. Resultant to this madness, nuclear, biological or chemical wars persistently loom large. It is reported that more than 100 million people were killed in the twentieth century in wars and civil conflicts,[1] and the new millennium opens with the terrorist attack of September 11.[2] Presently, the killing in the countries assailed by the ISIS is relentless- its toll is on the rise. It turns out that one violent century is taken over by another more violent century. With conflict raging the world and killings taking place on an unprecedented scale, reconciliation and peace are needed more than ever. In this regard, Genevieve Jacques aptly says:

> Never before has the themes of reconciliation been referred to so often as one of the priorities of our times. And no wonder, when one realizes the depth and magnitude of *the* consequence of the massive violations of human rights, inter-communal conflicts, hot and cold wars that have plague our world over

the last decades leaving in their wake broken bodies, broken minds, and broken relationship. Today's need for reconciliation of individuals, communities and nations are proportionate to the wounds caused by the violence that has ravaged their societies.[3]

While the two World Wars signify the outburst of generations of accrued conflicts, the formation of League of Nations in 1919 and the UNO (United Nations Organisation) in 1945[4] manifest the peoples' intensified need for peace and reconciliation.

It is no wonder that conflicts and its resultant bloodshed have penetrated the Kuki society like any other society of the world. For ages, the Kuki had their sovereign country under their abled chiefs and used all possible means to protect their sovereignty.[5] The dawn of Christianity in 1910[6] to the Kuki and their encounter with British colonial power were epochal. Christianity introduced Jesus Christ and the reconciliation brought by Christ to them. With its onset the Kuki, from head hunter turned to soul winner thereby bringing many to Christ. Contrarily, the British suppressive policy scattered the Kukis by dividing their country into different countries infringing upon their freedom. Reeling under the legacy of British 'divide and rule policy' taken over by the Indian government after its independence in 1947, the Kuki society continues to witness human rights violation, wanton killings, divisions and enmity down to the present day. A perusal of the various instances of conflicts in the modern Kuki society ascertains that reconciliation is right away required.

Genesis of Conflicts in the Kuki Society

Anglo-Kuki War 1917-1919

One dominant national ethos of the Kuki is their love of freedom- the freedom to do anything without interference. Such was their love for freedom that Kuki resistance against the British expansionist policy began in 1771,[7] and the last leg of the war was fought in 1917-1919.[8] Colonial writers termed the event as a rebellion arising out of the Kukis' refusal to enlist in the British Corps drive for France during the First World War.[9] However, to native scholars it was a war of independence. The imposition of house tax and the vesting of power to the *Lambus* (Hills peons) and Government Interpreters by superseding the power of the Chiefs put the independence of the Kuki at stake. When in between 1907-1917 an estimate of 1195 guns were confiscated the situation exacerbated. Consequently, the Kuki people took upon themselves the responsibility of defending their independence. They sought the alliance of the leaders of Bengali Nationalist Organization (BNO) who helped them set up an understanding with the Germans. The Germans supplied arms and ammunition to the Kuki.[10] Sadly for the Kuki, the war came to an end because of the depletion of their food resources.

Following the war, the British followed a policy of "disarming" the Kuki by confiscating arms and weaponry. Many of the Kuki Chiefs and leaders were either exiled or imprisoned in Sadiya in Assam, Taungyi Jail in Burma (Myanmar), and the Andaman and Nicober Islands.[11] The British assumed direct administration over the hill people especially, the Kuki chiefs. With the initiation of direct administration, three sub-divisional headquarters i.e. Tamenglong, Ukhrul and Churachandpur were established for the containment of the recalcitrant Kukis.[12] Through the Government of India Act, 1935, the Kuki came to be separated between British India and British Burma. The suppressive policies of British instigated the Kuki to take anti-British stance and fought alongside the Japanese force during the Second World War. As a result, the defeat of the Axis Powers came as a serious setback. The Kukis consequently came to be divided under the three newly independent nation states of India, Burma (now Myanmar), and East Pakistan (now Bangladesh). Ironically, to the dismay of the Kuki, the trifurcation took place in the absence and without the consent of the Kuki chiefs and the people.[13] This resulted in the "ethnification"[14] of the Kuki under the three countries. Then on, the Kuki became an "ethnified nationality" divided under the three newly independent states. The implication of which is that it led to their mobilization and consolidation into separate identities in relation to their geographical and political context i.e. Kukis in Manipur and other Northeast states, Mizos in Mizoram and Chins in the Chin Hills of Myanmar in the post independence period. Separated into different districts, states and countries estranged and violated everywhere; the Kukis took to demanding the restoration of their rights since the 1940's.

Emergence of Ethnic/Sub-Ethnic interest based organization

The introduction of Christianity, democratic institutions and spread of western education generated ethnic and political consciousness in the Northeast India. In keeping with the trend in Lushai Hills and Naga hills, in Manipur too, the Communist led by H. Irabot advocated the liberation of Manipur through the Maoist line of armed struggle based on "Meitei National Question".[15] Likewise, the Kukis also formed their own political organisation- the Kuki National Assembly (KNA) on 24 October, 1946. The primary objective of the KNA was to act as a pan Political organization amongst the Kuki tribes.[16] Since its inception, it was against the hill areas being merged with the Valley of Manipur and threatened secession. Though KNA projected a pan Kuki identity, it could not emerge as a common platform for all the Kuki tribes. Nor could it sustain her threats of secession due to internal conflicts amongst the Kuki-Chin tribes over the issue of identity and nomenclature. In more ways than one, the publication of William Shaw's *Notes on the Thadou-Kukis* had sown the seed of division among the Kukis. It puts the non-Thadou speaking Kuki tribes and clans[17] as subjects of the Thadous.[18] This invited a stiff resistance from the non-Thadous. A series of Meetings were held to solve this controversy but failed. On 28 June, 1947, the Khuga Valley Chiefs' Conference passed resolutions condemning Shaw's remark and denounced the identity "Kuki" on the ground that it was an imposed term. As an alternative organisation, Khulmi National Union (KNU) mainly comprising of the non-Thadous Kukis was form in July, 1947.[19]

The gap between the thadous and the non-Thadous widened when in accordance with the Manipur State Constitution Act, 1947 two ministers one each from the Naga and Kuki groups to represent the hill peoples in the Interim Council of the Manipur Government was to be nominated. The Naga instantly put up their candidate. However, Consensus eluded the Kuki group about their ministerial candidate. KNA by objecting the candidates put up by the Paite National Council and the Khulmi National Union[20] created widespread discontent amongst the non-Thadous group and the resultant growing popularity of KNU. However, KNU also failed to garner a mass support base amongst the Kuki-Chin tribes as the majority group Thadous did not support it.

KNU suffered another setback when the Constitution Scheduled Castes/Scheduled Tribe (SC/ST) Order, 1951 of the Government of India did not give recognition to the term "Khulmi" in the Scheduled Tribe list of Manipur. In Manipur the order mentioned the Scheduled Tribes list as (i) Any Kuki Tribe (ii) Any Lushei Tribe and (iii) Any Naga tribe. Therefore each Kuki tribes began to promote their own sub-ethnic and clan identities. When the Backward Classes Commission of India came to Manipur to review the SC/ST lists, each tribe demanded recognition. And as per the recommendation of the Commission, the term "Any Kuki" and "Any Naga" Tribes were omitted in the Government of India Scheduled Castes/Scheduled Tribes Lists Modification Order (Manipur), 1956. Instead twenty nine tribes were recognized as separate Scheduled Tribes in Manipur.[21] Thus the ground was set for the disintegration of the Kukis along their own sub-ethnic based identities. This led to the break-up of KNA and paved the way for the birth of Hmar Congress (HC) in 1954, Paite National Council (PNC) in 1956, Gangte Tribal Union (GTU) in 1958, Zou National Organization

(ZNO) in 1958 and Vaiphei National Union (VNU) in 1960.[22] Notwithstanding the inter-ethnic conflicts amongst the Kuki tribe over issues of identity and nomenclature, fear of valley domination and threat of Nagas also became apparent. In 1956 the Manipur Village Authority (Hill Areas) Act was passed by the Government of Manipur which bypassed the right of Kuki Chiefs over land. While such resentment against the Act was going on, in 1957 Manipur Naga Convention (MNC) was held at Ukhrul. The Convention proclaimed its solidarity to the Naga cause under Naga National Council (NNC). With this Naga armed activists began systematic campaign against the Kukis by imposing forced household taxes and carried out forcible occupations of Kukis' land as a part of their claims of the hill areas of Manipur as their ancestral land.[23] According to Goswami, within a decade i.e. from 1956-1964, the Naga armed activists devastated nearly 60 Kuki villages in Tamenglong and Ukhrul districts of Manipur.[24] Besides, due to the process of Nagaisation, many Old Kukis tribes [25] in Manipur who were closer to the Kukis linguistically and culturally disowned Kuki identity and joined the Naga fold.[26]

Demand for Sixth Schedule in Manipur

The growing autonomy aspirations of the hills people in Northeast India spurred the Constituent Assembly to incorporate the Fifth and Sixth Schedules to the Constitution of India as a form of autonomy arrangements for the protection of identity, culture and traditions of the hill tribes in the region. Despite this constitutional arrangement for the hill tribes of the region, the hill areas in Manipur were left out. Instead the hill and valley areas of Manipur were merged under a common unit of administration and hill administration came to be placed under the Manipur State Darbar under the provisions of the Manipur State Constitution Act, 1947. Since then the tribes have been administered through a series of acts and legislations from time to time.[27]

Subsequently, when Manipur was to attain its statehood, the Government of India proposed creation of six autonomous district councils[28] under the Manipur (Hill Areas) Autonomous District Councils, Act, 1971 to meet the autonomy aspirations of the hills people.[29] Accordingly, six Autonomous Districts Councils were constituted in the hill areas of Manipur by the Manipur (Adaptation of Laws) Order, 1972. However, as the envisaged District Council turned out to be not autonomous it met with widespread opposition. The Council members were to be appointed by the Governor and were to function under the Deputy Commissioner. Due to the inherent defects and anomalies, the hill tribes including the Kukis demanded for scrapping of the said Act, and insisted on the extension of the provisions of the Sixth Schedule in the Hill Areas of Manipur. In connection with this demand in its report submitted on 2002, the National Commission for Reviewing of the Indian Constitution had recommended for the extension of Sixth Schedule in the hill districts of Manipur. The State cabinet meetings have also endorsed the extension of the Sixth Schedule in the hill areas of Manipur for several times but with subject to "local adjustments" and "amendments". Finally, on 10 October, 2008, the Manipur (Hill Areas) District Councils (Amendment) Bill, 2008 was passed in the State Assembly. However, the Act is still opposed by the hill tribes on the ground of inherent defects and anomalies and continued the demand for the extension of Sixth Schedule in the hill areas.[30] The Sixth Schedule has continued to be a bone of contention between the hills and the valley. It is one of the causes of disunity and division in Manipur. The issue has brought suspicion, disunity, skirmishes, and disruption of normal life, and killings.

Towards an Armed Struggle

In 1965, in accordance with the Kawnpui Convention, the Kuki-Chin tribes have participated in the MNF movement led by Laldenga with a view to secure "Greater Mizoram". However, with the signing of the "Mizo Accord" between the Government of India and MNF, the concept of "Greater Mizoram" as envisaged in the "Kawnpui Convention" of 1965 failed. This led to dissension amongst the various Kuki-Chin tribes. Besides, the Accord also resulted in a security void in the face of increasing threat of Naga armed activists under the newly formed Naga armed group- Nationalist Socialist Council of Nagaland (NSCN). In its manifesto, the NSCN took up the agenda of Naga integration under one common political entity under "Greater Nagalim". Especially with the emergence of NSCN (IM)[31] systematic campaign against the Kukis by the Naga armed groups started in the form of collecting "Greater Nagalim" tax from Kuki villages and through threats and elimination of prospective Kuki leaders and Chiefs.[32]

Thus the failure of the "Mizo Accord" to address the issue of "Greater Mizoram" and the increasing threat of

Naga armed groups under the NSCN (IM) paved the way for the emergence of armed organisation in the latter half of the 1980s with demands for creation of a separate "Kuki State" within the Indian Union. On 18 May, 1988 the Kuki National Front (KNF) was formed under the leadership of Nehkholun Kipgen at Molnoi in the Indo-Myanmar border. It strives for the creation of a separate "Kuki state" within the Indian Union.[33] In the same year, on 24 February, the Kuki National Organisation (KNO) and its armed wing KNA (Kuki National Army) were formed at Molnoi under the leadership of Thangkholun Haokip. The KNO strives for self-determination of the Kuki both in India and Myanmar within a "defined territory".[34]

Kukis' Retaliation in Self-defence against the NSCN (IM)

The sporadic clashes between the Kukis and the Nagas turned into full scale ethnic clash in June 1992. The Nagas view the Kukis as aggressor who attempt to capture the land of the Nagas. The Kukis on their part assert their views of being the indigenous people who for the protection of their land had fought the imperialist British invasion in 1917-1919.[35] The Kuki Inpi Manipur (KIM) circulated its disapproval of the use of the terms such as "ethnic conflict" or "ethnic clashes" and clarified that it was an "ethnic cleansing" carried out by the NSCN (IM) since the 1950s.[36] Unable to bear the sustained killing of their people, the Kukis began to retaliate in self-defence.[37] With the birth of KNF and KNO, the Nagas became more apprehensive of the Kukis and began to view the Kukis as a threat to their demands for "Greater Nagalim". On 22

October, 1992 the UNC on its "Quit Notice" to the Kukis, asked them to vacate their lands by December 1992. This eventually led to full blown ethnic killings and claimed more than one thousand lives from both communities.[38] However, Wati is of the view that the Kukis were the first to serve the "Quit Notice" to the Nagas at Moreh and the Nagas in retaliation ordered the Kuki to leave their lands.[39] Regardless of who perpetrated the conflict, the Kukis suffered more casualties with a loss of 905 lives,[40] 360 villages destroyed, 100, 000 people displaced[41] and 207 Nagas were killed.[42] From the hindsight knowledge, it is apparent that the colliding political interests and the claim of land ownership were behind the bloodshed between the Naga and the Kuki. Sadly, no official pact has yet been signed between the two, though the killings subsided by 1997 and had taken the form of sporadic clashes then on.

Kuki-Zomi conflict

Following the ethnic cleansing disaster, the Zomi movement gained momentum in Manipur especially among the Paites. The movement was based on the assumption that the correct name of the Kuki-Chin is Zomi.[43] While the Kukis retaliation to the Nagas was in full swing, in 1993 Zomi Revolutionary Organisation (ZRO) was formed with an aim to promote Zomi identity and political interest. With the formation of Zomi Revolutionary Army (ZRA) in 1997 as its armed wing the Paites began to oppose their inclusion in the Kuki nomenclature.[44] The formation of ZRA and its alleged nexus with the NSCN (IM) came to be increasingly viewed by Kuki armed group like KNF as a threat. On the other hand, ZRA became apprehensive of the presence of Kuki armed groups and increasing migration of Kuki population from other areas into Churachandpur. Armed clashes started between KNF and ZRA which consequently led to the killing of 9 persons and injuring 4 others belonging to Paite community at Saikul village on 24 June, 1997.[45] This incident was followed by senseless fighting, killings, arsons and destruction of properties between the two communities. The situation was put under control by the intervention of the State Government. On 1 October, 1998 a memorandum of understanding was signed between the Kuki Inpi[46] and Zomi Council.[47] However, the conflict has created a wide gulf between the two communities so much so that unity is still elusive as both sides are apprehensive of each other and the diverging political pursuits persistently continue.

Kukis' Resistance Against the Meiteis' Persistent Annexation of the Hill Areas

The various policies and legislations of the Government of Manipur in her post-statehood created a sense of discrimination; exploitation and domination among the hill people. With a view to implement uniform land laws both in the hills and valley of Manipur, the Government based on Meitei interest has been trying to extend the Manipur Land Revenue and Land Reforms Act (MLR and LR) Act, 1960 in the hill areas through the MLR and LR (Amendment) Act, 1975. In the face of their growing population, the Meiteis in Manipur have an eye for the hill areas. However, the hill tribes- the Kukis and Nagas regarded it as a plot to do away with the rights of the tribal chiefs over land ownership. More significantly, in order to protect the integrity of Manipur,

Manipur Peoples' Liberation Front (MPLF) was formed as a conglomeration of the Meitei armed groups. Since then, 33 innocent Kuki have been killed, maimed, injured and displaced due to the landmines planted by valley based constituent armed groups of the MLPF- especially the United Liberation Front (UNLF) to thwart off security forces from Kuki areas in Chandel district and Churachandpur district. In January 2006, the UNLF indulged in mass gang rape of 21 Hmar women at Parbung and Lungthulien villages, Tipaimukh which prompted 1000 Hmar villagers in the area to flee to Mizoram.[48] Again on 13 May, 2007, 400 Kuki villagers were taken as captives inside Myanmar.[49] All these forms of human rights violations of the Kuki people consequently resulted in armed clashes between the UNLF and KNA which spill-over to civil population claiming the lives of three Kukis and six Meiteis on 9 June, 2007 at Moreh, a border town in Manipur.[50] While the KNO alleged the conflict in Moreh as a result of UNLF's illegal intrusion into Kuki territory and demanded that it should confine its ideology and politics within the limits of Imphal valley, the UNLF on the other hand branded the KNA as communal force acting in collusion with the Indian security forces. Such occasional conflicts between the armed groups of the two communities added to the already fragile ethnic situation in the State.

The Internecine Killing

In their initial years of formation, both Kuki National Front (KNF) and Kuki National Army (KNA) took up a protracted armed struggle against the security forces of India and Myanmar to press their respective demands. However, splits began to occur in both the armed organisation giving a serious setback to their movement. After the death of Nehkholun Kipgen in 1993 a leadership crisis ensued leading to the formation of KNF (Military Council). On the other hand, in December 1995, after the assassination of Thangkholun Haokip by his own dissenting group, KNA (Military Council) was formed. However, it was soon disbanded. Thus, the ground was set for formation of more splinter groups. In 29 December, 1999 a group of dissenters again defected from KNF (Military Council) and formed the Kuki revolutionary Army (KRA) under the leadership of Khuplam Hangsing. Another two more factional groups- KNF (Zougam) and KNF (Samuel) have emerged from its parent organisation. In early 2000, following an election debacle, another Kuki armed organisation United Kuki Liberation Front (UKLF) was formed.[51] Over the years owing to internal contradictions and leadership crisis several factional and new Kuki armed groups have come up.[52]

Soon, the Kuki society began to witness the mushrooming factional groups. Internal rivalries, struggle for power and the control of territories led to factional clashes between the different splinter groups even in public places. In 2003, the presence of KNA in some parts of Kangpokpi district and Kuki inhabited area of Ukhrul district provoked KRA. Killings between the two rival groups ensued. On 7 January 2005, KNA cadres waylaid and kill one cadre of KRA at Molnom village.[53] On 12 January, 2005 Khaimang Haokip, the commander in chief of KNA was killed by the alleged combined force of UKLF and KRA at Bijang, Churachandpur.[54] Consequently, Khuplam Hangsing was killed at his hide-out in South Delhi in 2007. On 9 June 2008, 2 KNA cadres and 1 KRA cadre were killed during a factional clash between the two outfits at Molkon village in Kangpokpi district. The formation of UKLF in early 2000 was also followed by the fratricidal killings between UKLF and KNA. The clashes between the two splinter groups continued till UKLF took control of Pallel area, Sugnu area and Dingpi area of Chandel district. In Churachandpur area, the internecine clash between KNF (Military Council) and KNF (Samuel) resulted in the killing of 3 cadres belonging to KNF (Samuel) on 4 April, 2005.[55] Due to the inter-factional killings, the Kuki people live in incessant fear and insecurity. The society is now divided on the line of clans, sub-tribes and factional groups. The struggle for territorial control and resources has taken precedence over the welfare of the people.

Conclusion

The Kukis, sandwiched between the political aspirations of the Meitei and the Naga, and the internal conflicts live in perpetual fear, nightmare and agony. This has not only affected its socio-politico-economic dimensions but also has tremendously impinged on the spiritual spheres of the People. As a result, many began to question the Christian faith they profess. Relentlessly, ethnic competition and conflict between the Nagas, Meitei and Kuki intensify in Manipur. Thus, Manipur witnesses an ethnic cauldron- the Kukis for "Kuki Homeland" or "Zalengam" and the Nagas for "Greater Nagalim" while the Meiteis are apprehensive of losing control of Manipur. The situations worsened with the unprovoked internecine killings. It comes to the surface that different aspiration and different struggle of different people is at the core of the conflict situation of the state and the Kuki society.

In the backdrop of this volatile ethnic situations in the state, and the internecine clashes between the Kuki armed groups, reconciliation and peace are of utmost need for the Kuki in Manipur. It is at this juncture that one wonders, how the Kukis sustain their society. Despite the carnages tearing the society apart from the inside, the Kukis have their traditional practices of reconciliation and conflict resolution. In order to throw more light on the issue, the following Chapter examines the Kuki traditional concept and practice of reconciliation. In doing so, the Kuki people and their historical background, polity, traditions and religious practices need to be adumbrated alongside.

Endnotes

[1] Robert J. Schreiter, *The Ministry of Reconciliation* (Bangalore: Claretian Publication, 1998), 3.

[2] Michael Jansen, "The Terrorism Trap" *Sunday Herald*, 15 September 2002, 4, cited by Lipoknungsang, "Toward a Contextual Theology Of Reconciliation in the light of the concept and practice of *Aksu* among the Ao Nagas" (M.Th. Thesis, Senate of Serampore college, 2003).

[3] Genevieve Jacques, "Communicating Reconciliation: The Churches Responsibilities in an Increasingly Secular Society," in *Media Development*, XLVII/ 4 (2000): 29.

[4] Anil Chandra Banerjee, *An Outline History of the World* (Calcutta: A. Mukherjee & Co., Private Ltd., 1969), 246.

[5] Lhunkhotong Doungel, *Chin-Kuki Bulpi Phunggui Thusim Leh Chondan Bu* (Imphal: Guite Doungel council, 1993), 77. Hereafter cited as Doungel, *Phunggui Thusim Leh Chondan Bu…*

[6] M. Thongkhosei Haokip, *Ecumenism Among the Kukis of North East India* (Secunderabad: Published by the Author, 2016), 68. Hereafter cited

as Thongkhosei Haokip, *Ecumenism Among the Kukis of North East* India...

[7] Gangumei Kabui, "Genesis of the Ethnoses of Manipur," in *Manipur, Past and Present: The Ordeals and Heritage of Civilisation*, vol. 3, edited by Naorem Sanajaoba (New Delhi: Mittal Publication, 1998), 34.

[8] *Brief Notes on Kuki Nation* (Imphal: Kuki Organisation for Human Rights, 2013.), 2. Hereafter cited as *Brief Notes on Kuki Nation*...

[9] L.W. Shakespeare, *Guardians of the Northeast: The Assam Rifles 1835-2002* (Shillong: Directorate General of Assam Rifles, 2003), 15.

[10] P.S. Haokip, *Zalengam: The Kuki Nation* (Zalengam: Kuki National Organisation, 2008), 146. Hereafter cited as P.S. Haokip, *Zalengam: The Kuki Nation*...

[11] Aheibam Koireng Singh and Pryadarshini M. Gangte, *Understanding Kuki since Primordial Times: Essays by Late Dr. T.S. Gangte* (New Delhi: Maxford Publications, 2010), 76-80.

[12] T.S. Gangte, The *Kukis of Manipur* (New Delhi: Gyan Publishing House, 1993), 10. Hereafter cited as Gangte, The *Kukis of Manipur*...

[13] Interview with T. Lunkim, Administrative Secretary Kuki Christian Church, Imphal, 18 October 2016.

[14] "Ethnification" refers to the "process through which the link between territory and culture is attenuated, and the possibility of a nation sustaining its integrity is put into jeopardy". One variant of this process may take place through the division of a given ethnic group's ancestral homeland into two or more states, thereby endangering their integrity as nations. See, T.K. Oommen, *Citizenship, Nationality and Ethnicity: Reconciling Competing Identities* (New Delhi: Polity Press, 1997), 13.

[15] Naorem Sanajaoba, "The Genesis of Insurgency," in *Manipur: Past and Present*, vol. 1, edited by Naorem Sanajaoba (Delhi: Mittal Publications, 1988), 245.

[16] T. Tongkholun Haokip, "The Kuki National Assembly: The Party's Role in the State Politics of Manipur" (M.Phil. dissertation, NEHU, 1993).

[17] The tribes include Gangte, Vaiphei, Hmar, Chiru, Changsan, and Lunkim.

[18] William Shaw, Notes *on the Thadou-Kukis* (Guwahati: Spectrum Publications, 1929), 124.

[19] Ashok Kumar Ray, *Authority and Legitimacy: A Study of the Thadou-Kuki in Manipur* (New Delhi: Renaissance Publishing House, 1990),

115-116. Hereafter cited as Ray, *Authority and Legitimacy: A Study of the Thadou-Kuki*...

[20] T.T. Haokip, "Kuki Armed Opposition Movement," *Eastern Quarterly* 6/ 1 (Spring and Monsoon, 2010):27.

[21] Kuki Tribes like Aimol, Chiru, Gangte, Hmar, Kom, Maring Paite, Simte, Sukte, Vaiphei and Zou were given separate recognition. See, Seikhogin Haokip, "Genesis of Kuki Autonomy Movement in Northeast India," in *The Kukis of the Northeast India: Politics and Culture*, edited by Thongkholal Haokip (Delhi: BOOKWELL, 2013), 56. Hereafter cited as Seikhogin Haokip, *The Kukis of the Northeast India*...

[22] Ray, *Authority and Legitimacy: A Study of the Thadou-Kuki*...124-125.

[23] Seikhogin Haokip, *The Kukis of the Northeast India*...59

[24] Ratna Tikoo, "Ethnic Issue in North-east India: An Overview in Manipur," in *Political Dynamics of North-east India*, edited by Girin Phukan (New Delhi: South Asian Publishers, 2000), 219. Hereafter cited as Tikoo *Political Dynamics of North-east India*...

[25] The tribes include Aimols, Anals, Chothes, Chirus, Kharams, Lamkangs, Marings and Monsangs

[26] Lal Dena, "The Kuki-Naga Conflict: Juxtaposed in the Colonial Context," in *Dynamics of Identity and Intergroup Relations in Northeast India*, edited by Kailash S. Agarwal (Shimla: Indian Institute of Advanced Studies, 1999), 186.

[27] Some of the important Acts and Legislation for administering the affairs of the tribals in the hill areas include Manipur Hill Peoples(Administration) Regulation Act, 1947, the Manipur Village Authority (Hill Areas) Act, 1956, the Acquisition of Chief Rights (Hill Areas) Act, 1967 and the Manipur Land Revenue and Land Reform Act (MLR and LR), 1960.

[28] The proposed six districts council under the Manipur Hill Areas District Councils Act, 1971 are: Manipur North ADC now Senapati ADC, Sadar Hills ADC, Manipur East ADC now Ukhrul ADC, Tengnoupal ADC now Chandel ADC, Manipur South ADC now Churachandpur ADC, Manipur West ADC now Tamenglong ADC.

[29] Rajendra Kshetri, *District Councils in Manipur: Formation and Functioning* (New Delhi: Akansha Publishing House, 2006), 16-17.

[30] Seikhogin Haokip, *The Kukis of the Northeast India*...61-63.

[31] The NSCN was formed by a group of Naga dissidents who did not approve the "Shillong Accord" under the leadership of Th. Muivah, Isaac Chisi Swu and S.S. Khaplang.

[32] P.S. Haokip, *Zalengam The Kuki Nation*...305.

[33] Nehkholun Kipgen, "Why not Kukiland for Kukis," in *Ahsijolneng*, edited by Jamkhohao Touthang (Shillong: KSO Shillong, 2007), 18.

[34] P.S. Haokip, *Zalengam The Kuki Nation*...402.

[35] A. Wati Longchar, "A Case Study of Naga-Kuki Ethnic Violence and Peace Initiative," *Journal of Tribal Studies: Tribal Ethics VI/* 2 (July-December 2001): 101-102. Hereafter cited as Wati, *Journal of Tribal Studies...*

[36] *Traditional Policy and Political Stand Point of Kuki Inpi* (Imphal: Kuki Inpi Manipur, 1995), 1.

[37] P.S. Haokip, *Zalengam The Kuki Nation*...303.

[38] Kiranshankar Maitra, *The Noxious Web: Insurgency in the North-East* (New Delhi: Kanishka Publishers, 2002), 164.

[39] Wati, *Journal of Tribal Studies*...102.

[40] P.S. Haokip, *Zalengam The Kuki Nation*...303.

[41] *Brief Notes on Kuki Nation*...11.

[42] Wati, *Journal of Tribal Studies*...105.

[43] "Zo" is believed to be the common ancestor of the Kuki-Chin tribes and "mi" means people. Therefore "Zomi" colloquially refers to "Zo people". See, Thangkhangin, "Prism of the Zo People," in *Souvenir of 60th Zomi Namni Celebration*, edited by Thangkhangin (Lamka: Publication Board 60th Zomi Namni Celebration Committee, 2008), 201-210.

[44] Rebecca. C. Haokip, "The Kuki-Paite Conflict in the Churachandpur District of Manipur," in *Conflict Mapping and Peace Process in Northeast India*, edited by Lazar Jeyaseelan (Guwahati: North Eastern Research Centre, 2008), 187. Hereafter cited as Rebecca, *Conflict Mapping and Peace Process in Northeast India...*

[45] Rebecca, *Conflict Mapping and Peace Process in Northeast India*...192.

[46] Kuki Inpi is the apex political body of the Kuki and regarded as Kuki government.

[47] "Final Peace Accord between Zomis and Kukis for Restoration of Peace and Normalcy," signed on 1 October, 1998 at Churachandpur, 1.

[48] *The Sangai Express* (Imphal) 13 June, 2007.

[49] Press Release of the Kuki Students' Organization, Delhi (KSO-D), 23 March, 2007, New Delhi.

[50] *The North-East Sun* XII/23 (July 1-15, 2007): 24.

[51] Seikhogin Haokip, *The Kukis of Northeast India...*69.

[52] The groups include Kuki Revolutionary Army (Unification), United Kuki Liberation Army (Military Council), Kuki Revolutionary Front (KRF), Kuki National Liberation Front (KNLF), Zomi Revolutionary Army(ZRA), United Socialist Revolutionary Army(USRA), Zomi Revolutionary Front(ZRF) and Komrem Peoples' Revolutionary Army(UKRA).

[53] Interview with Khuppao Khongsai, Chief of Molnom village, Ukhrul district Manipur, 16 October 2016.

[54] *The Imphal Free Press* (Imphal), 13 January 2005, 1.

[55] *The Imphal Free Press* (Imphal), 5 April, 2005, 2.

Chapter - 2

Hemkham -
Its Implication in the Process of
Reconciliation in the Kuki Society

The Kukis are historically well documented and politically disconsolated lots. They were known for their unity under the leadership of their abled chiefs. Gradually, due to rapid conversion into Christianity, spread of education, employment opportunities, and search for education, the Kukis began to move towards greener pastures.[1] As a result, erosion of their traditions, cultures and customs gradually started. In the post independence era the Kuki society is marked by a downward drift in all walks of life. Weakened and disunited so much so that they have come to be termed as "nomad" in their own land.[2] As such, the defence of their land, identity, and the consequential entanglement in the web of ethnic competition becomes their hallmarks.

The imbroglios that encompass the society intensify the Kukis' predicament. However, in the flagrant conflict situations and the killings therein, the Kukis sustain their society by their traditional practice of conflict resolution and reconciliation. In order to deal with the Kuki traditional practice of conflict resolution and reconciliation, the knowledge of Kuki people, their historical background, polity and religious practice is a prerequisite. Therefore, the focus of this chapter will be the Kuki people- tradition and culture, and their practice of conflict resolution and reconciliation.

Ethnography of the Kuki

The Kukis are a group of ethnic communities belonging to the Kuki-Chin linguistic group.[3] They inhabit the contiguous areas of North east India, Northwest Myanmar and the Chittagong Hill Tracts of Bangladesh. In Northeast India, they are found in the states of Manipur, Assam, Nagaland, Tripura, Mizoram and Meghalaya. However, predominantly they settle in Manipur i.e. in Churachandpur district, southern parts of Chandel district, Tengnoupal district, Kangpokpi district, western parts of Tamenglong district and south-eastern part of Ukhrul district. They constitute one of the three ethnic groups in Manipur besides the Meitei and Naga.[4]

The word "Kuki" is a generic term which includes a number of tribes and clans. This generic term covers a large number of people who migrated to different parts of Northeast India from contiguous areas lying further east at different points in time.[5] There are many conjectures and theories about the origin of the word "Kuki". Some believed that this had been derived from the Baluchistan word "Kuchis" meaning, "wandering people". Some others viewed that it comes from English word "Kooky" which means peculiar or unusual people. It was perhaps used as a derogatory name given by the outsiders to an ethnic group of people living in the western Myanmar, Northeast India and Bangladesh. They are a sub-family of the Tibeto-Burman or Indo-Chinese family.[6] Sadly, the Kuki in the present day usage is distinct from the Kuki of antiquity which represents the ethnic whole. The usage of the term is narrowed down to the Thadou speaking group of the erstwhile Kuki nomenclature. However, depending on where they settled, the acceptance on the part of the people of other cognate tribes to the usages of the term 'Kuki" in several places cannot be denied entirely.

Socio-cultural life

Tucha and *Becha*

The basic traditional practices essential to the Kuki are the institutions of *tucha* and *becha*. It is through them that the family units maintain close relationship between the families of different clans. *Tucha* simply refers to the nephew/niece born of a sister/sisters or daughter/daughters. *Tubul*[7] is chosen preferably from the offspring of the sisters followed by the daughters' sons. The *tucha* under the command of the *tubul* and direct supervision of the *becha* see to it that the entire work connected with all sorts of social functions and ceremonies, such as the preparation of a feast and liaison works are carried out. *Becha* is a person nominated by the ego to represent him in connection with all the social functions and ceremonies.[8]

Becha can best be understood as the alter ego of the *ego*. By extension of the terminology it can be nominated from a wide range of people, including good and reliable friends of non-consanguinal relatives. The *becha* is the spokesperson of the ego on a self reciprocal basis and is the administrator with his full authority to exercise discretion on behalf of the ego.[9] The *tucha* along with the *becha* thus become the entourage of the *ego* in the performance of any social functions, ceremonies and fulfilment of any social obligations.

Khankho[10]

Khankho is a whole ethical principle of the Kuki by which each Kuki is bound of his/her social and political obligations in the society. It has a close resemblance to *Tlawmngaihna* of the Mizo and *Sobaliba* of the Ao-Naga. It is the role and obligation with which each Kuki is bound to and expected of. Each set of rules applied to a household is applied to the village, clan, and tribes and beyond. The father has his role and obligation so as the mother and the children within the family. They as a family have obligation to the extended families and these families to the clan, village, and tribes and further. Upon this faithfulness to the *Khankho*, the Kukis' understanding of "loving your neighbor as yourself" is built and faithfully performed.[11]

Khankho involves respect, sacrifice, obedience, and reciprocal obligation for the welfare of the society. It denies self-interest and keeps no polarity between the rich and the poor, men and women, and powerful and the weak. Though based on reciprocal obligation *Khankho* is never meted out in expectation of reciprocity. It is based entirely on selflessness.

Religious life

The Kuki people from their ancient past lived in the forests and adapted themselves with ecology and environment. Interaction with varied situations, phenomena beyond their wisdoms and grasp had attuned them to believe in the existence of supernatural beings. The Kukis believed in the existence of god called *Chung-Pathen*, considered to be a High or Supreme God. He is believed to be the highest benevolent God who lives in heaven or sky. *Chung-Pathen* is the Creator and Sustainer of the universe and all the living beings. They firmly believed that everything concerned with prosperity, growth and strength in life are the free gifts of *Chung-Pathen*. The Kukis believed in the sovereignty and omnipotence of *Chung-Pathen*. They believed that *Chung-Pathen* seldom interferes in the daily affairs of human beings, nor does he demand sacrifices of appeasement and placation from the people.[12] However, the wrath of God against injustice and *chonset* (sin) and the prevalent of sacrifice and offerings of penance could be gathered from some of the traditional practices.

The concept of *Chung-Pathen* is abstract and thus it has no anthropomorphic form or a permanent place or residence. Besides, the reign of other deities or evil spirits which were behind the evils in the world was believed by the Kukis. In order to appease the evil spirits elaborate rituals and sacrifices which constitute *phuisam*[13] were solemnised by the *thempu*.[14] This dread and fear of the endless spirits and the consequential performance of elaborate rites and rituals became their religion.

Polity

A village is an independent political unit among the Kukis, and the Chief of the village and his Council of Ministers are the political leaders. Administrations of justice, enforcement of executive function, maintenance of social practices and customary law, including religious performances are within the jurisdiction of the village Chief and his Council of Ministers.[15] The hearing of all the cases and village meetings take place at the residence of *Haosa* (village chief), and this might be the reason why a village court is known as *Haosa* Court. The land and other properties, both movable and immovable, are owned by *Haosa* for the whole village. Chieftainship is hereditary and the Chief usually is the *Upa* (Head genealogically) of a clan. However, *Semang Pachong* (Council of Ministers) is nominated from among the villagers by virtue of their merits. Beyond the village, *Inpi* a conglomeration of *Haosa* take care of the administration. The administration of a *Lhang* (area) is attended by *Lhang Inpi* (Area chiefs' Association). The issues involving different villages, areas, tribes, communities and nations fall under the jurisdiction of the *Kuki Inpi* (Kuki Government). *Kuki Inpi* is the apex body of the Kukis. The traditional *Kuki Inpi* which remained latent for many years was revived during the 1980s and 1990s.[16] The portfolios and power in chiefdom were traditionally dignified with the spirit of selflessness in service and dedication.

Kuki Traditional practice of Conflict resolution and Reconciliation

Salam-Sat

Adultery and fornications are serious offences in the Kuki society. As such, fornicator and adulterer are held in low esteem. As a blot to the family, clan and village this immoral act spurs a bloody retaliation. In order to prevent the repercussions, intervention of *Haosa* is sought. In the case of an unmarried girl being impregnated, the boy who is responsible for the act is asked to take the girl as his wife. However, the refusal on the part of the boy to take the impregnated girl as his wife obligates him to perform *Salam-sat* a customary law pertaining to adultery. On the ground of devastating the chastity of the girl and defamation, a *sel* (Mithun) is to be given by the boy as fine. On the refusal of the impregnated girl to be taken as wife, the girl would bear and deliver the child and nurture it for about three years. At the expiry of the stipulated period of time, the boy is handed his child after he gives the girl a *sel* (mithun) and a *dah* (Myanmarese gong).[17]

In the case of a wife indulging in adultery, all ties with her husband are severed through divorce and sent back to her parent's. However, in the case of rape, the rapist kills a pig at the court of the *Haosa*. Besides, a *sel* (mithun) is incurred from the *upa* (usually eldest brother) of the rapist's family as a penalty for defaming the victim's family.[18]

Toltheh

Normal quarrels in the Kuki society are considered natural, but once bloodshed is involved, the case is heard in the court of *Haosa*. In case of any bloodshed, the case of shedding blood is promptly taken up pending the hearing of the case. The person who sheds blood has to perform *Toltheh* as ordered by the *Haosa*.[19]

Toltheh literally means sweeping ground but the practice and concept of *Toltheh* symbolises the purification of the village ground defiled by the shed blood. The perpetrator is ordered to kill a boar and set a jar of *ju* (rice beer) for the *Haosa* and his *Semang Pachong*. The boar and the jar of *ju* are fine imposed for such act which is independent of the claim that is to be made by the injured at the hearing of the case.[20]

Once the case is settled, after a stern warning by the *Haosa*, the perpetrator has to bear the cost of treatment. On the full recuperation of the injured, a feast is to be arranged by the perpetrator's family to convey that the victim has been healed. This feast partaken by the two families including their *tucha* and *becha* is known as *Ankong-Sokhom*. In case of bloodshed during an attack of the victim at his/her residence, a *sel* (mithun) has to be given to the victim by the attacker. Such attack is an insult and requires a fine of *sel* to appease the wrath of the victim's family and relatives who could still be crossed.

Hemkham

In the Kuki society, if a person is killed either by accident or with a premeditated motive, *Hemkham* is performed.

Hemkham literally cannot be translated. Made up of a combination of two words, *hem* means "sharp" as in the case of a sharp weapon, and *kham* is paradoxically pregnant with meanings, literally. The English equivalence of the word *kham* can best be understood in the combined meaning of the words- stop, ban, halt, prevent, evade and cease. Kipgen, literally translated *Hemkham* as "preventing sharp weapon".[21] To Satkai Chongloi, *Hemkham* is like the present day cease-fire.[22]

Given its rich meaning, *Hemkham* can best be understood as the traditional concept and practice of the Kukis, performed to prevent retaliation or any act of vengeance as a reaction to killing/murder. It is performed through the intervention of *Haosa* and the liaison of the *Thempu* in order to reconcile the two hostile groups involved.[23]

The performance of *Hemkham,* as a result brings about the evasion of the use of weapons that can inflict further harm and aggravate the hostility wrought out by the killing. *Hemkham* prevents any retaliatory actions from the deceased side, at the same time; it puts in check the continued possible infliction from the killer's side. An evasion of the use of weapons is solemnised with the motive to reconcile the two hostile groups. This performance renews and restores friendship, comradeship and unity in the society.

Hemkham –Its Concept and Practice

The concept and practice of *Hemkham* revolves around the evasion of retaliation with the aim of reconciling the two hostile groups involved in a bloodshed by offering and killing a *Vohchal-tuhnga* (a boar measuring five palms breath). It symbolises a sacrificial act of penance.[24] This performance allocates blood as the core of life and acknowledges the value of life. It implies that the blood sheds in the killing/murder contaminates the village, ground, land and the society thereby requires purification to evade the wrath of God, who is against such act, and the consequent bloody retaliation from the victim's side and the possible continue assault from the killer's side.

On a given day, a *Vohchal-tuhnga* for *Ankong-sokhom* (feast) has to be offered on behalf of the culprit at the residence of the *Haosa*. A placing of a jar of *ju* before the *Haosa* and *Semang Pachong* precedes the killing of *Vohchal-tuhnga*. The *tucha* under the command of *tuchabul* and direct supervision of the *becha* engaged themselves in the preparation of the feast.[25] Out of the killed *Vohchal-tuhnga*, pieces of meat are cut off as *saba*[26] which would be distributed to the participants of the hearing of the case which followed *Ankong-sokhom*. Best effort is exerted in the preparation of the feast because *Ankong-sokhom* is possible only if the deceased's side, after the persuasion of *Haosa* agrees to partake. The feasibility of the *Ankong-sokhom* is a sure sign of the anticipation of reconciliation by both sides. Once the blood of *Vohchal-tuhnga* is shed and *Ankong-sokhom* takes place, retaliation from the deceased's side and enmity between the two hostile groups are evaded and reconciliation takes place.[27] As the outcome of *Hemkham* another *Ankong-sokhom* is arranged by the culprit on a given day, which is known as *Chamna-satha*.[28] After the hearing of the case and a settlement is reached, the culprit has to compensate for the loss to the next and kin of the deceased by giving the following items: two *khichong* (beads) to compensate for the eyes, one d*ah* (Myanmarese gong) for the pillow, one *pondum* (blue shawl) for shrouding the mortal body and one *sel* (mithun). However, the settlement of the case would be different in the case of an accidental killing. A more lenient settlement is sorted out for accidental killings depending on the demand of the deceased's side.[29]

The proceeding of *Hemkham* begins with a *phuisam* by the *Thempu*. *Haosa* is the judge and the hearing of the case takes place in the presence of the deceased's representatives-*tucha, becha* and the *upa* (eldest sibling of the deceased) and other elders, the same is required from the culprit's side. *Semang Pachong* assists *Haosa* in the settlement of the case.[30] The discretion of *Haosa* when attested by the *phuisam* of the *Thempu* has a religious sanctity.[31]

As such, the verdict of *Hemkham* is considered as the verdict of God and a breach of *Hemkham* is never thought of.[32] Any breach of *Hemkham* tantamount to incurring the wrath of God, the entire village and clan. It is believed that the violator becomes a prey to all sorts of evil due to the sanctity of *phuisam*.[33]

Procedures of Hemkham

In performing *Hemkham*, certain procedures are followed. The gravity of the crime demands a thorough analysis and a maximum participation. As such, efforts are made so that all those who are entitled to be at the hearing of the case are not left out. Being a sensitive issue, participation of the majority is essential for striking a bilateral settlement.[34] Depending on the jurisdiction, the place of the hearing of the case and the participants are sorted out. Representatives from both sides are equally important. They are to put up their case and take a pledge on behalf of the people involved in the killing.

Hemkham at the village level

A bloodshed involving persons of the same village is within the jurisdiction of the village *Haosa*. In this case, *Haosa* of the village in which the killing takes place has to intervene. The killing of the *Vohchal-tuhnga* and the hearing of the case usually takes place at his residence. The *upa* (eldest brother) of the deceased along with his *tuchas* and *bechas* and other principal members of the deceased's family represent the deceased. The same people from the side of the culprit represent the culprit.[35] In most cases, the culprit is excluded for security reason. In the presence of these people from both sides, *Thempu*, *Haosa* and *Semang Pachong*, the performance of *Hemkham* at the village level takes place.

Hemkham at the Clan level

In the case of bloodshed involving persons belonging to different clans, *phung upa* (head of clan) of both sides have to be involved. *Tucha, becha, upa* (eldest brother) of both the deceased and other responsible members from both sides are to participate in the performance of *Hemkham*. The killing of *Vohchal-tuhnga* is held at the court of the *Haosa* (village Chief) of the deceased. *Ankong-sokhom* followed and the process culminated in the hearing of the case and final settlement.[36] The *phung upa* (head of the clan) takes the place of the eldest brother of the deceased and speak and pledge for the on behalf of the deceased. The same is true of the culprit.

Hemkham involving two Villages

The performance of Hemkham involving two villages would necessitate the intervention of the Lhang Inpi. The Haosa of both the two villages have to represent the deceased and the culprit respectively. In this case, Hemkham has to be performed at the residence of the Haosa of the deceased's village. However, the residence of the Haosa is temporarily accepted as the court of the Lhang Inpi. Inpi Pu (President of Lhang Inpi) judges the case. The participation of both the Haosa are essential by the virtue of the sovereignty that each of them possess. The other participants are the same as in the case of Hemkham at the village level and clan level.[37]

Hemkham involving other tribes

In case of a Kuki killing a person or being killed by a person belonging to other tribes, the intervention of Kuki Inpi and that of the apex body of the other tribe is sought. In this case, Kuki Inpi represents the person belonging to Kuki community. If the deceased belongs to other tribes, Kuki Inpi performs Hemkham and fulfils the demand made by the deceased's side. In the case of the deceased being a Kuki, the head of other tribe has to perform Hemkham and is bound by the customary law. As such, payment of the items ingrained in the customary law of Hemkham has to be made. The items paid could be made symbolically in cash and kind. In this case, Vohchal-tuhnga will not be imposed; any four legged animal killed for the occasion would be accepted as Vohchal-tuhnga.[38]

Hemkham- Its Implication in the process of Reconciliation

The traditional practice of *Hemkham* is still in vogue among the Kukis and their cognate tribes. It is through the practice of *Hemkham* that reconciliation is sought and peace is restored in the society. The hostility, suspicion, distrusts, and the strained relationship resulting from the killing which could lead to another spree of reckless killing is evaded by this practice. The Kuki society as mentioned in chapter 1 experienced conflicts which resulted in wanton killings. In fact, on many occasions, the impending killings of retaliation were stopped by the performance of *Hemkham*. The following incidents elucidate the performance of *Hemkham* and its effectiveness:

Hemkham between Kuki and Zomi

The Kuki and Zomi though cognate tribes have differences on issues pertaining to nomenclature and political aspirations. The long simmering differences flared up when KNF mowed down ten persons belonging to the Zomi community. As a result, brutal killings, destruction of properties and arsons followed on an unprecedented scale. The situation disturbed peace and tranquillity of the state as both sides were constantly on the look-out for the next preys. Headed by Nipamacha Singh, the Chief Minister of Manipur, a State High Level Committee (SHLC) was formed.[39]

At the behest of SHLC and the authorisation of Kuki Inpi and Zomi Council *Hemkham* was performed. KNF, as the perpetrator offered a bull for the *Ankong-sokhom* on 29 September, 1998. The performance of *Hemkham* was followed by *Chamna-satha* and another *Ankong-sokhom* on

30 September, 1998. Final agreement was signed between Zomi Council and Kuki Inpi on 1 October, 1998.[40] Since then normalcy and peace returned to Churachandpur district.

Hemkham between KNF and KRA

In the late 1990s Kuki National Front (KNF) and Kuki revolutionary Army (KRA) comprising of various clans were involved in internecine killing. Bloodshed, loss of lives, attacks and counter attacks took place as a result. In order to prevent further killings and reconcile the two groups, *Kuki Inpi* intervened. At the command of *Kuki Inpi*, *Hemkham* was performed at Kuki-*In*[41] between KRA and KNF on 9 April, 2001. Following the traditional practice, tea was served in place of *ju* and *Vohchal-tuhnga* was killed for *Ankong-sokhom*. *Saba* was given to the head of every principal clan who represented his clan and those representatives of the various social organisations.[42] The internecine killings between KNF and KRA stopped thereafter as a result of the performance of *Hemkham*.

Hemkham between Kuki and the Meitei

On 22 December, 2009 two Kukis[43] who were students of North Eastern Hill University (NEHU) Shillong were lynched by Meitei belonging to Nongbram village, Thoubal district, Manipur. The two were mistaken as members of a Kuki armed group who were alleged to have attacked the village. The following day as a sign of protest against the killing of the Kuki Students' Organization (KSO), All Naga Students 'Association Manipur(ANSAM), Kuki Movement for Human Rights(KUMHUR) and Kuki Women Union(KWU) imposed bandhs on NH-39 connecting Imphal and Dimapur. The killing had spurred tension in the state as retaliation was in the offing from the Kuki side. In order to prevent the exacerbation of the situation *Hemkham* was performed on 31 December, 2009 with the intervention of the Government of Manipur.[44] The meiteis from Nongbram village being the culprits killed a *Vohchal-tuhnga* and arranged *Ankong-sokhom* at the *Haosa* court of Bongbal Kholen. The meiteis were represented by leaders of United Clubs of Manipur (UCM) and All Manipur United Clubs' Organisation (AMUCO). The Kukis were represented by *Kuki Inpi* Manipur (KIM).

Hemkham between Kuki and the Government of Manipur

On 1 September, 2004 Jangkholen Chongloi of Khongsai Veng, Imphal was pulled out of his house and shot dead in front of his family members by the Manipur Police Commandos. As the news of the killing spread, the Kukis in Imphal and beyond fumed with anger to the extent of steering a riot. Before the matter went out of control, the Government of Manipur intervened by sending two emissaries in the persons of Ngamthang Haokip (Cabinet Minister) and Francis Ngajokpa (Cabinet Minister). Manipur Government performed *Hemkham* by killing *Vohchal-tuhnga* followed by *Ankong-sokhom* at the residence of Khongsai Veng *Haosa*. The leaders of Kuki Students' Organization and the Kuki Movement for Human Rights (KUMHUR) represented the deceased.[45]

Misappropriation of *Hemkham*

The practice of *Hemkham* is in currency effectively in the Kuki society. However, the practice of *Hemkham* taking the multi-cultural and pluralistic view into consideration has not followed its pristine format in its entirety. This alteration has gone to the extent that despite making *Hemkham* relevant, this new trend resulted in the misappropriation of the concept and practice of *Hemkham*. In the present format the religiosity formally attached to it has been downplayed. *Hemkham* now becomes purely a secular and judicial affair denunciating its religious sanctity. In contrast, the concept and practice of *Hemkham* used to be equivalent to a religious ceremony and the participation of *Thempu* to solemnise the performance was quintessential. On this line, the performance of *Hemkham* encompassed both the secular and spiritual's sphere. Presently, despite Christian concept of reconciliation having a strong influence among the Kuki Christian, the concept and practice of *Hemkham* remain outside the purview of the church. As a result, *Hemkham* remains to be seen as a heathen practice and the involvement of the church is neglected. Consequently, the fallacy brings about polarization between the two i.e. *Hemkham* for secular realm and Christian reconciliation for spiritual sphere. The polarization on its part hinders the acceptance and development of a holistic view of *Hemkham* and the implication of Christian reconciliation in the Kuki society.

Besides, the fear of the performance of *Hemkham* being dictated by extraneous forces and biasness on the part of the *Haosa* cannot be ruled out down-right. However, this does not equate the performance of Hemkham as entirely bias and distorted. On the other hand, every effort is exerted so that justice prevails and reconciliation is achieved in the performance of *Hemkham*.

Apparently, the Kuki Society has a rich concept and practice of conflict resolution given the web of conflicts pervading it. In fact, the various forms of conflict resolutions to reconcile the antagonistic groups have helped the society to court back peace and normalcy in the society. As stated earlier, different forms of conflicts and crimes are meticulously tackled by different performances of penance. With the gravity of the crime the penalty intensified and killing being the most heinous crime is solved by the concept and practice of *Hemkham*.[46]

However, despite the religiosity attached to *Hemkham*, no attempt has yet been made to see it through the periscope of Christianity. Moreover, no attempt has been made to contextualize Christian concept of reconciliation from the Kuki perspective. A keen observation of the Kuki society juxtaposes to the Christian concept of reconciliation reveals that synthesizing *Hemkham* with that of Christian reconciliation is necessary and equally viable. The synthesization of the two will help in the formulation of a contextual theology of reconciliation from a Kuki perspective which would enrich both the concepts. In order to contextualize the concept of reconciliation in the Kuki society through the concept and practice of *Hemkham*, the next chapter will deal with traditional Christian concept of reconciliation.

Endnotes

[1] T.S. Gangte, *The Kukis of Manipur*...223.

[2] The *Sangai Express* (Imphal) 28 October, 2016, 1. Also see, *Poknapham* (Imphal) 28 October, 2016, 1.

[3] G.A. Grierson, *The Linguistic Survey of India*, vol. III, part III (Calcutta: Government Printing Press, 1904), 4.

[4] P.S. Haokip, *Zalengam: The Kuki Nation*...23.

[5] Gangumei Kabui, *History of Manipur: Pre-Colonial Period*, vol. 1(New Delhi: National Publishing House, 1991), 23.

[6] Sonthang Haokip, "The Erstwhile Territorial Domain of the Kukis," in Kuki *Society: Past Present Future*, edited by Ngamkhohao Haokip and Michael Lunminthang (New Delhi: Maxford Books, 2011), 45.

[7] *Tubul* denotes the head among the *tucha*.

[8] Interview with Hemkhothang Baite, Chief of Litan Sareikhong, Ukhrul District Manipur, 6 October 2016. Hereafter cited as Interview with Hemkhothang Baite...

[9] T.S. Gangte, The *Kukis of Manipur*...132.

[10] Literally, *khan* means behavior, *kho* means a village.

[11] Satkhokai Chongloi, "The Unseen Christ among the Kuki people," in *Garnering Tribal Resources For Doing Tribal Christian Theology*, edited by Razouselie Lasetso (Jorhat: ETC Programme Coordination, 2008):176-177.

[12] T.S. Gangte, The *Kukis of Manipur*...161.

[13] *Phuisam* means incantation.

[14] *Thempu* served as the priest in the pre-Christian Kuki society.

[15] T.S. Gangte, The *Kukis of Manipur*...125.

[16] T. Lunkim, *Kukigam Nam Kivaipohna leh Kuki Christian Houbung* (Imphal: Published by the Author, 2016), 7-8.

[17] Interview with Thangkhojang Baite, Chief of B. Phaicham, Churachandpur District Manipur, 28. September 2016. Hereafter cited as Interview with Thangkhojang Baite...

[18] Chongloi, *Peacemaking in the North East India*...103-104.

[19] Kipgen, *Garnering Tribal Resources*...76

[20] Interview with Hemkhothang Baite...

[21] Kipgen, *Garnering Tribal Resources*...77.

[22] Satkhokai Chongloi, *Peacemaking in the North East India*...104.

[23] Interview with Jamchon Baite, Village Secretary of B. Phaicham, Churachandpur District Manipur, 6 June 2016. Hereafter cited as Interview with Jamchon Baite...

[24] Interview with T. Lunkim, Administrative Secretary Kuki Christian Church, Imphal, 18 October 2016.

[25] Literally *ankong* means plate but denotes a meal.

[26] *Saba* is a portion / piece of meat given to the principal participants of *Hemkham* as a sign of being one of the witnesses. Those who receive *saba* are expected to exercise their moral responsibility to ensure that the two contracted parties keep the injunction of *Hemkham* pronounced by the *Haosa*.

[27] Interview with Hemkhothang Baite...

[28] Literally, *chamna* means peace and *satha* means killing of an animal. Thus *Chamna-Satha* involves killing of *vohchal-tuhnga* or other four legged animal for the feast of Peace.

[29] Kipgen, *Garnering Tribal Resources*...77.

[30] Interview with Hemkhothang Baite...

[31] Interview with Jamchon Baite...

[32] Interview with Hemkhothang Baite...

[33] Interview with Nehlhun Baite, Church Elder of T. Lailoiphai Village, 3 November 2016. Hereafter cited as Interview with Nehlhun Baite...

[34] Interview with Thangkhojang Baite...

[35] Interview with Hemkhothang Baite...

[36] Interview with Jamchon Baite...

[37] Interview with Nehlhun Baite...

[38] Interview with Hemkhothang Baite...

[39] Interview with Thangkhojang Baite...

[40] "Final Peace Accord between Zomis and Kukis for Restoration of Peace and Normalcy," signed on 1 October 1998 at Churachandpur, 1.

[41] *Kuki-In* is a community Hall of the Kukis located at Old Lambulane, Imphal.

[42] Kipgen, *Garnering Tribal Resources*...77-78.

[43] The victims were Paolenlal Chongloi of Keithelmanbi Military Colony and Paokhosat Kipgen of Bongbal Kholen. Satkhokai Chongloi, *Peacemaking in the North East India*...105.

[44] Satkhokai Chongloi, *Peacemaking in the North East India*...104.

[45] Interview with Lhunthang Mangte, Khongsai Veng, One of the Participants in the performance of the *Hemkham*, 17 October, 2016.

[46] Interview with Hemkhothang Baite....

Chapter - 3

The Traditional Christian Understanding of the Theology of Reconciliation

In the preceding chapter, attempt has been made to expound reconciliation as it is realized through the practice of *Hemkham* in the Kuki society. Following this, attempt will be made to analyze the traditional Christian understanding of the concept of reconciliation. All is not well in the relationship between God and humankind is the inherent idea of the concept of reconciliation. Human beings succumbence to sin distorted the relationship between husband and wife (Adam and Eve), between siblings (Cain and Abel), in the community (Tower of Babel) and between humanity and the natural world (Gen. 3:17-19; 4:10-12; 9:1). Consequently, "God was in Christ reconciling the world to himself" (2 Cor. 5.19) summarizes what the Christian accepts as the solution.[1] Reconciliation is the heart of Christian message, and thus the heart of Christian doctrine or teaching is presented through it in the most sensible way understood by Jewish and Christian believers in a series of changing historical contexts.[2] Hence, this chapter will portray the traditional Christian concept of reconciliation across the ages.

What is Reconciliation?

In Christian doctrine, the word 'reconciliation' carries a range of meaning and is used with many connotations. Often, it is used to express the sum total of what Christians believe about God's saving work in Jesus Christ. At different places, reconciliation is interchangeably used with 'salvation', 'redemption', or atonement. Reconciliation can be understood as a renewal of trust after a period of hostility and conflict. Interestingly, the meaning and understanding of reconciliation can be extended to refer to peace-making between conflicting groups, communities, institutions or nations.[3] James H. Cone understands reconciliation as human fellowship with God made through God's activity in history, by setting people free from economic, social and political bondage.[4] Gutierrez holds it to be the breaking of all molds, a paradigm which sets the terms for a new order of human relationships wherein the "nobodies" who have no place become the centre-stage.[5]

On this line, reconciliation is a process of restoring relationship between two warring groups in order to bridge the gap of misunderstandings and hostility. At the same time, it involves a long-term process, an effort to build bridges of understanding.[6] In order to garner more understanding of the definitions of reconciliation, the biblical understandings of reconciliation need to be taken into account.

Biblical Understanding of Reconciliation

The Concept of Reconciliation in the Old Testament

The Old Testament does not specifically mention the word "reconciliation" but the concepts corresponding to reconciliation are mostly discussed under "Atone." The problem of a broken relationship between God and the human race because of sin brought about an objective guilt and alienation which must be covered or removed if fellowship is to be restored.[7] On this line, Sin in the Old Testament is understood as a breach of Covenant obligation. As the outcome of sin, sacrificial system was designed to 'atone' these sins. Yet, there is no exact word for reconciliation in the Old Testament comparable to the function of "reconcile" and "reconciliation" in the New Testament.[8] No word in the Old Testament corresponds directly to the New Testament word *Katallassein* meaning "to reconcile".[9] Indeed, Hebrew word, *kaphar* meaning 'to atone,' "cover" and to 'ransom' is closest in meaning to reconciliation. *Kaphar* is used in ritual, especially sacrifice. For instance, in Leviticus chapter 6 the expression of "to make atonement" (v.3) is made. In 8:15 of the same book, Moses is portrayed as pouring out the rest of the blood at the base of the altar and consecrated it "to make atonement for it". The same act of penitence by a priest is found in the second book of Chronicles 29:24. Besides, the use of *Kaphar* outside of rituals is seen in Noah's building of the ark, where the structure is "covered" with pitch, and the name of the lid of the ark is *kappored,* which means "cover" or "place of atonement". In few cases, *kaphar* is used to express human's relationship as in the case of Jacob and Esau in

Genesis 32:20. Jacob says, "I may appease (*akapperah*) him (Esau) with the present that goes before me, and afterwards shall see his face; perhaps he will accept me". *Kaphar* also appears in 2 Samuel 12:3 on the same thought.[10]

In sacrificial ritual, *kaphar* is the means to achieve reconciliation. For example, atonement in Exo.30:11-16, is a monetary "ransom" payment in which the blood is "the price for (ransoming) the soul" of the person who offers it.[11] And Lev. 17:11 explains the reason for the ancient Israelites restriction to eat the blood of any fellowship offering animals; "for the life of a creatures is in the blood, and I have given it to you to make atonement for yourselves on the altar; it is the blood that makes atonement for one's life."[12] Despite the numerous related words in the Old Testament such as redemption, forgiveness, and pardon 'atonement' concept of *kaphar* in the Old Testament is closest to the idea of reconciliation in the New Testament. *Kaphar* serves as a firm foundation for the New Testament concept of reconciliation as both are concerned with the relationship between God and human being, and between human and human.

The New Testament Concept of Reconciliation

Reconciliation in the New Testament concept is the restoration of the relationship between human beings and God. God exerts the reconciling power as human being is alienated from God; living "without God" on their own resources and deprived of hope (Eph. 2:12).[13] This alienation can also be viewed as the consequence of sin, and for that reason expiation of sin effects reconciliation. To Paul's understanding, sin is an objective state in which humankind finds themselves, even estranged from their own choice.[14] In the Gospels, Jesus Christ richly used Reconciliation or its related terms. For example, Jesus preaches repentance (Mk. 1:14). He also tells parables of reconciliation with God (Lk. 18:10-14) and reconciliation with the community (Matt. 9:1-8).

In the act of reconciliation, God is the prime mover because God commends his own love to us while we were yet sinners and that Christ died on our behalf (Rom. 5:8). God sets him forth as expiatory, through faith, by his blood (Rom. 3:25). The effect of Christ's death and resurrection is to remove a state of enmity between God and human being. And through the Cross the enmity is slain, and Jews and Gentiles are reconciled to God and to each other in one body (Eph. 2:16) The state of hostility, which is so closely related to the law of commandment in ordinances is abolished in His flesh through death (Co. 1:22), through Him all things reconciled, for He has made peace through the blood of His Cross (Co. 1:20).[15]

Pauline concept of Reconciliation

There are around 11 instances of the term reconciliation in the New Testament, out of which 10 come from Paul's letter. The word *Katallasso* is found three times in Rom. 5:10; 2 Cor. 5:18-20, and 1 Cor. 7:11. *Katallasso* is compound of *allasso*, to alter, exchange meaning to reconcile. In the New Testament, *Katallasso* occurs only in the sense of to reconcile, or (passive) to be reconciled. It is used to denote reconciliation of human with one another. The corresponding noun is *katallage* found in Rom. 5:11; 11:15; 2 Co. 5:18-19 which means reconciliation. The subject of the reconciliation is God (2 Cor. 5:18ff). This is a theological novelty compares to non-Christian religious thoughts, in which the deity is a mere object of the reconciling work of human. The *katallage* created by God is thus, a completed act which precedes all human actions. "For if while we were enemies we were reconciled (*katallagemen*) to God by the death of his son… we are reconciled (*katallagentes*) shall we be saved by his life" (Rom 5:10). The word *apokatallasso,* which means to reconcile is found in Col. 1:20, 22; Eph. 2:16. Ephesians 2: 11ff, talks about the breaking down of the "dividing wall of hostility" between Jews and Gentiles.[16] S.E. Porter opines "Reconciliation is a Pauline concept in which enmity between God and humanity, or between human groups, is overcome and peaceful relations restored on the basis of the works of Christ".[17]

To add to this, Pauline letters offer a more thematized outline of the theological dimension of the term reconciliation. Paul stresses on humankind's alienation, estrangement, and indeed hostility to God and the subsequent reconciliation effected by God. Four principal texts highlight the key elements of reconciliation in Pauline doctrine: The first thing which arrests the attention is the meagre use of the three Greek words which directly express the idea of reconciliation. They are found only in the Pauline Epistles i.e. 1 and 2 Corinthians, Romans, Colossians and Ephesians.[18] 'or else be reconciled to her husband' (1 Cor. 7:11) illustrates the use of the passive form *katallage* (reconciliation) of a relationship in which active co-operation is implied.[19] On the whole, the New Testament *katallage* (reconciliation) is a legal term used with husband and the wife as in Cor. 7:11, and thus deals with personal relations i.e. the end of hostility and the restoration of friendship.[20] For example, the woman is not expected to be inert in her attitude to the proposed reconciliation. In 2 Cor. 5:18-20, God reconciles humankind to God's own self through Christ by not holding humans' sins against them. Romans 5:10-11 implies that Christ's death is the means whereby God destroys the hostility; Colossians 1:20-22 talks about Christ's death as the means whereby peace is made, although there are two ambiguities, where it is God or Christ who acts and whether the peace is between God and creatures, among creatures, or probably both. Christ, by his death, restores friendship with God by breaking down the walls of separation among people, with the Jew-Gentiles distinction, so radically divisive for the early church, the archetype of how change takes place and what humans are freed from.[21]

The Pauline material further projects the attention to several theological understanding of reconciliation. Firstly, the reconciliation between God and the human race is achieved through the forgiveness of sins (II Cor. 5:18-20, Colossians 1:20-22). God takes the initiative and sets aside the imbalance of power between creator and creatures by humbly becoming incarnate and even more humbly by accepting death to establish humans in a relationship with God (Philippians 2:5-11). The key theological understanding of reconciliation expresses it in term of the mystery of salvation i.e. God's gratuitous justification of humans.[22] For these reasons, it is clear that Paul based his understanding of reconciliation on the reconciliation between God and the human race.

Secondly, Paul understands reconciliation as the reconciliation between communities, namely the Jews and the Greeks/Gentiles (Ephesians 2:11-16).[23] The primary purpose of the breaking down of 'the middle wall of partition' was to create in Christ the one new being by making peace and reconciling them into one body into God through the cross, thereby ending the enmity'.[24] Soukup in this regard asserts that, within the history of Christianity, this reconciliation was experienced as an open communication between individual members of the two communities (Peter and Cornelius in Acts 10). But for Paul it denotes a wider communication between Jews and Greeks in the Christian communities in Philippi, Corinth, Rome, and so forth.[25]

Thirdly, Paul describes the reconciliation between individuals and the community and in so doing, seems to echo the Gospel instruction in Mathew about fraternal correction. This situation involves a specific kind of reconciliation where one confesses one's sin and is forgiven.[26]

Fourthly, Paul understands reconciliation as reconciliation between individuals in the community between husband and wife. 1 Cor. 7:11 discusses the issue of divorce; "to the married I give you charge not I but the Lord, that the wife should not separate from her husband but if she does, let her remain single or else be reconciled to her husband (*e to andri katallageto*) and that the husband should not divorce his wife. In this regard, reconciliation does not create something new, but restores the relationships to its normal form.[27] The Pauline passages reveal that friendship, forgiveness and reconciliation are gifts from God. These are necessary to restore humankind's relationship with God as well as with other fellow human beings, because God has forgiven human beings and reconciled them through his sacrificial works, requiring the forgiveness of one another.

Reconciliation in the History of Christian Theology

Reconciliation in the Theology of Early Church

In the patristic period, baptism was regarded as the chief locus of reconciliation by the church fathers. Peder Nogard is of the view that Karl Rahner Stressed on the importance of baptism as the means for reconciliation.[28]

Reconciliation was intimately associated with Baptism and was understood as the sacrament of forgiveness. It was understood not only as the forgiveness of sins but also as the incorporation into Christ who had overcome "the powers and principalities, the spiritual hosts of wickedness". Baptism was believed to seal a person for eschatological salvation, and the Eucharist was the celebration of the incorporation into the salvatory Mystery by becoming a member of the eschatological community.[29] And the inextricable interrelationship between the sacrament of baptism and unity was never static.[30] Further, it reflected an individual's experience of the forgiveness of sins and a new birth to holiness and reconciliation with God in baptism. At the same time, the individual entered into the community and experienced reconciliation with others. Later on, practical necessity of forgiving and reconciling those who were separated from the community/church due to apostasy or other serious offences led to a penitential practice that involved both ritual and public penance.[31]

Any person cut off from the community/church by serious sins could enter the order of penance only once. The process involved asking prayers of the community, confession of faith in God's mercy and acknowledgement of sin, doing public penance, alms-giving and a public ritual of reconciliation.[32] In this way, the theological focus of reconciliation shifted to the individual; followed by the communicative focus, in which an individual's contact with the community was restored through the process.

The Eighth century witnessed different theological understandings of personal reconciliation. Celtic monastic practice gradually spread throughout the western churches to be disrupted by two significant changes:

Firstly, it was believed that reconciliation could be celebrated as often as needed and it took place privately. It was then that, private penances were taken up according to the nature and severity of the sin.[33] The form of post-baptismal reconciliation emphasized the relationship between the individual and God. Besides, its growth from monastic origins, coupled with the interpersonal emphasis of the direction of souls dominated and led to a more private theological understanding of reconciliation.[34]

Secondly, in both the Patristic and Celtic forms, penitents had to do some acts of penance, and the focus was restoration of relationship (communication) with the community. For the purpose, payment of some kind could replace the penitent's acts of satisfaction in substitution for payment of a punishment. While Patristic Mediterranean practice had focused on exclusion from Eucharistic communion and public penance as a sign of repentance, the Celtic one moved to private, individual confession of sins and acts of satisfaction. As the outcome, reconciliation came to encompass private forgiveness, satisfaction, and justification.[35] Resultantly, medieval theology of Christ's work as redeemer that stressed 'satisfaction' emerged. This on its part led to a theology of sacramental reconciliation. Anselm of Canterbury gave a theological expression that set the stage for the late medieval and reformation debates about the relation of justification and reconciliation.[36]

Reconciliation in Medieval and Reformation theology

During the medieval phase, Anselm of Canterbury (1033-1109) profoundly influenced Western Christianity in the assumption that God's honour and justice were violated by human sin requiring an offering of satisfaction before God, so that God could forgive human beings and be declared righteous. However, as no form of penance was adequate, it was fulfilled by the God-man Christ. He assumed the burden of human guilt and the punishments which followed, namely death, and made it possible for God to be God to exercise grace.[37]

For centuries, the understanding of reconciliation continued to emphasize more on the rituals than to the act of God in Christ. In order to avoid the danger of Pelagianism the late medieval theologians considered the ritual and the reality of reconciliation as a balance between God's freedom and human action. However, by twelfth and thirteenth centuries, theologians agreed that sacramental reconciliation involved the four elements of contrition, confession, satisfaction and absolution, all in response to God's grace.[38] On this line of thought, Thomas Aquinas said that, the three "parts" of the sacrament-contrition, confession, and satisfaction-were the *matter* and that the absolution was the *form*. He stressed the efficacy derived from the form and the significant of the sacrament form the matter. The absolution communicated the fruits of Christ's passion to the penitent, as the penitent cooperated with grace in the destruction of sin. Coming to confession was a sign of the sinner's will to be converted, and the absolution could change attrition to contrition and thus positively affect the forgiveness of sin.[39] On Aquinas' thought, Poschmann commented:

> The great and epoch-making achievement of Aquinas' teaching on the penance was the integration of the sacrament in the process of justification, and consequently the proof that it was an indispensable cause of the forgiveness of sin.[40]

However, the debate on the subject of penance continued for a considerable length of time. Given the supreme importance of the forgiveness of sins and reconciliation with God in Christ through faith, it was not surprising that this issue was at the core of the Protestant Reformation. Indeed, the first two of the Luther's Ninety-five Theses attached the institution of sacramental penance, denying that it was what the Lord meant when he said' "Repent!" Luther proclaimed instead that only faith enabled men and women to appropriate the righteousness God gracefully attributed to them in Christ.[41]

Luther's theological understanding of reconciliation took justification as its point of departure. Unlike the scholastic theologians, for Luther, Christ through his mediations between

God and humankind brought "which was absolutely necessary for human beings... through his priestly work he protects humankind from all sins and the wrath of God, intercedes for them, and sacrificed himself in order to reconcile humankind to God."[42] Through his work humankind become his own and are so ruled by him that he gives humankind a share in his life in "righteousness, innocence, and blessedness" which is his lordship.[43] In Geneva under Calvin, something similar to the old public penance was administered by the civil magistrates, and divine worship contained a general confession of sin and a declaration of pardon. Calvin regarded private confession, either to a pastor or to a fellow-Christian, as something salutary but by no means necessary. Confession might be valuable for the correction of the sinner, the quieting of an uneasy conscience, or reconciliation among Christians, but Calvin did not regard it as in any way sacramental.[44] For Zwingli, frequent confession to God was an integral part of Christian life; but confession to another Christian, except for the purpose of advice, was of no particular value.[45]

Following this, the council of Trent (1545-1563) rejected any compromise with the Reformation and emphasized penance as true sacrament. The necessity of confession and its divine institution as deriving from the power of the keys was proclaimed.[46] Thus, in the wake of the Reformation, the Council of Trent drew up rules called the sacrament of Confession.[47] Further, absolution was held to be a judicial act and not merely declaratory, and the sacrament of penance as an efficient cause of the forgiveness of sins was canonized. The Council also set forth a Rite of Penance incorporating this view with minor modification, and was used in the Roman Catholic Church until the liturgical reforms of the Second Vatican Council. Ironically, Christendom remained divided for four hundred years over the essential matter of reconciliation with God in Christ.[48]

Reconciliation in the Contemporary Theology

The questions of sacramental reconciliation did not occur much in Post-Reformation Protestant theology. However, following Luther, the ritual of private confession was not held as a 'sacrament in the same sense as the sacraments of baptism and the Eucharist'. In the ritualized reconciliation, Lutheran Church bore Christian witness to Christ's power within the church to isolate, repel, and negate sin.'[49] Later in the eighteenth and nineteenth centuries liberal Protestantism used the image of reconciliation to describe the action of grace; and expressed that, in so doing, it comprehended a subjective and more explicitly communicative model. "Forgiveness represented a change of heart through which God draws human beings away from guilt, sin, ignorance, egoism and isolation into a relationship with God."[50]

In the twentieth century, two significant elements dominated the theological discussion on reconciliation. Firstly, it made a community a more conscious dimension. Bonhoeffer pointed out that a 'community of peace' depends on the forgiveness of sins. The forgiveness of sins still remains the sole ground of all peace, even where the order of external peace remains preserved in truth and justice.[51] He returned to a New Testament understanding that reconciliation comes only as consequences of the forgiveness of sins.[52] Forgiveness characterized full life in community and leads members of the community to initiate the divine action by forgiving one another. Reconciliation was reconciliation both with God and with one's neighbour. The revised ritual of reconciliation stressed the reconciliation not only with God but also with the church. The assembled community was not merely present in an observing way, but the assembled community was present in participative way. As such the assembled community was an agent of reconciliation.[53]

Liberation theology extends reconciliation with a strong emphasis on the social nature of sin, an insight into the sinful structure of the world, and the discovery of human co-optation by the language of the oppressed.[54] In tune with this thought, Gustavo Gutierrez postulates three levels: (i) the socio-political level, i.e. liberation of the oppressed; 'exploited classes, despised ethnic groups, and marginalized cultures', (ii) the anthropological level: liberation for qualitatively different society with a human dimension; (ii) the theological level: liberation from sin, the ultimate root of all injustice and oppression, for a life of community and participation. The responsibility of theology of liberation is to go through these levels and articulates them in a differentiated account.[55] Thus, Liberation theology takes under its purview the social sins and economic evils as the basis for the disorders and hostilities, especially in the Third World and therefore, reconciliation must necessarily attend to these problems.

Secondly, contemporary theology broadens the understanding of reconciliation by considering its wider sacramental nature. Any ritual of reconciliation practiced by the church points both to church as a sacrament of reconciliation and to 'the Christ event as reconciliation event', in other words, all reconciliation takes root in Jesus, the primordial sacrament of reconciliation. When this sacramental process is applied to reconciliation we see that the church in its true essence must reflect the forgiving love of God, which one sees in Jesus, the light of the nations. Thus, the reconciliation celebrated by the church indicates the reconciliation that Christ has achieved.

Thus, God's forgiveness urges those forgiven to live in harmony with God, with one another, and with all creations. This view portends the New Testament material where reconciliation is seen in terms of relationship with God and with the community. The theological understandings of reconciliation expand on an anthropological view, principally by introducing a dependency on Christ. Christian reconciliation refers to Christ as source, as model and as motivation. Over the centuries, theological reflection has understood reconciliation literally, metaphorically and sacramentally.

In the light of what has been expounded, human beings, due to disobedience severed all ties with the Creator and within themselves. But God restored the relationship by sending the son, Jesus Christ. In doing so, God entrusted those reconciled to him to work for reconciliation in the context where killings, suffering and enmity have distorted the relationship God established through Jesus Christ.

In God's reconciliation lies humans' ministry of reconciliation. God liberates humans to let them partake in God's initiative to liberate; and God renews and empowers them so that they become a channel of God's new life in this world.[56] Thus, "reconciliation" which bridges nations, communities and individuals becomes inevitable for every individual to commit to be reconcilers and God's instruments as peacemakers. Consequently, Christians are ordained for the ministry of reconciliation. In the next chapter, attempt will be made to propose the concept and practice of *Hemkham* for the formulation of a contextual theology of reconciliation from the Kuki perspective.

Endnotes

[1] Colin E. Gunton, ed., *The Theology of Reconciliation* (London: T &T Clark Ltd., 2003), 1.

[2] John W. De Gruchy, *Reconciliation Restoring Justice* (Minneapolis: Fortress Press, 2002), 45.

[3] V. M. Sinton, "Reconciliation," *New Dictionary of Christian Ethics and Pastoral Theology,* edited by David J.Atkinson & David H. Field (Leicester, England: Inter-Varsity Press, 1995): 724.

[4] James H. Cone, "Theological Reflection on Reconciliation" in *Christianity in Crisis*, 32/24, (22 January 1973):305.

[5] Gustavo Gutierrez "Freedom and Salvation" in *Liberation and Change: The Death and Resurrection of the American Dream*, edited by Ronald H. Stone (Atlanta: John Knox Press, 1977), 35.

[6] Sydney D Dailey, *Peace is a Process: Swarthmore Lecture 1993* (London: Quaker Home Service and Woodbrooke College, 1993), 126.

[7] B.W. Bromiley, "Reconcile, Reconciliation," *The International Standard Bible Encyclopedia* Q-R, edited by Geoffrey Bromiley et al., vol. 4 (Grand Rapids, Michigan: William B. Eerdmans Publishing company, 1988): 55. Hereafter cited as Geoffrey Bromiley, *"Reconcile, Reconciliation"*...

[8] James Leo Garrett, *Systematic Theology: Biblical Historical and Evangelical*, vol. 2 (Grand Rapids, Michigan: Eerdmans Publishing Company, 1995), 302.

[9] The concept of Reconciliation or something equivalent to it is explicitly found 18 times in the whole Bible, out of which it is found only 7 times in the Old Testament. Even in these 7 times, the word 'reconciliation' is not used in those instances. See Carroll Stulmuellerr, C.P. "Reconciliation," in *The Bible Today* 79 (October 1975): 484.

[10] S. T. Kimbrough, Jr., "Reconciliation in the Old Testament," in *Religion in Life* XLI/1 (Spring 1973): 40.

[11] Richard E. Averbeck, "kpr," *New International Dictionary of Old Testament Theology and Exegesis*. vol. 2, edited by William AVan Gemeren et al. (Cumbria: Paternoster Publishers, 2002): 695. Hereafter cited as Richard E. Averbeck, *New International Dictionary of Old Testament Theology...*

[12] Richard E. Averbeck, *New International Dictionary of Old Testament Theology...*693.

[13] Andrew T. Lincoln, *Word Biblical Commentary, Ephesians*, vol. 42 (Dallas: Word Books, Publisher, 1990), 125.

[14] Geoffrey Bromiley, "Reconcile, Reconciliation"...17.

[15] G.W.H. Lampe, *Reconciliation in Christ* (London: Longmans Green and Company, 1955), 29.

[16] James D.G. Dunn, *The Theology of Paul the Apostle* (Grand Rapids: William Eerdmans Publishing Company, 1998), 228.

[17] S.E. Porter, "Reconciliation," *Dictionary of Paul and His Letters*, edited by Gerald F. Hawthorns, Ralph P. Martin and Daniel G. Reid (Leicester: Intervarsity Press, 1993): 695.

[18] Vincent Taylor, *Forgiveness and Reconciliation: A Study in New Testament Theology* (New York: Macmillan and Company Ltd., 1941), 71. Hereafter cited as Taylor, *Forgiveness and Reconciliation...*

[19] Paul A. Soukup, SJ, "Theological Understandings of Reconciliation," in *Media Development* XLVII/4 (2000): 25. Hereafter cited as Soukup, "Theological Understanding of Reconciliation"...

[20] Soukup, "Theological Understandings of Reconciliation"...26

[21] Soukup, "Theological Understandings of Reconciliation"...28.

²² Ralph P. Martin, *Reconciliation: A Study of Paul's Theology* (Atlanta: John Knox Press, 1981), 3. Hereafter cited as Martin, *Reconciliation: A Study of Paul's Theology...*

²³ Martin, *Reconciliation: A Study of Paul's Theology...*160.

²⁴ Taylor, *Forgiveness and Reconciliation...*76-77.

²⁵ Soukup, "Theological Understandings of Reconciliation"... 27.

²⁶ H.G. Link, "Reconciliation," *The New International Dictionary of New Testament Theology*, vol.3: Pri-Z, edited by Colin Brown (Devon: Paternoster Press Ltd., 1978), 172. Hereafter cited as Link, "Reconciliation,"...

²⁷ Link, "Reconciliation,"...172.

²⁸ Peder Nogaard-Hojen, "Baptism and the Foundation of Communion," in *Baptism and Unity of the Church*, edited by Michael Root and Risto Saarinen (Michigan: WCC Publications, 1998), 63.

²⁹ Frank C. Senn, "Structures of Penance and the Ministry of Reconciliation," *The Lutheran Quarterly* XXV/3 (August 1973): 270.

³⁰ J. Jayakiran Sebastian, "Baptisma unum in Sancta ecclesia," in *A Theological Appraisal of the Baptismal Controversy in the Work and Writing of Cyprian of Carthage* (Verlagander Lottbeck: Peter Jensen, 1997), 33. Hereafter cited as Jayakiran, *A Theological Appraisal of Baptismal....*

³¹ Penance is the ministry of reconciliation placed at the service of church discipline. Thus, the object of penance at its deepest level is the reconciliation of lapsed Christians with God through Christ in his Church. See *Works of Martin Luther*, vol.1 (Philadelphia: Muhlenberg Press, 1915), 17.

³² Peter Michael Hansell, "Why was the Shepherd of Hermas left out of the New Testament Canon? A Contextual Study in Church History and its Contemporary Relevance," *Bangalore Theological Forum* XXXIV/ 2 (December, 2002): 42-43.

³³ Hyde, *To Declare God's Forgiveness: Toward a Pastoral Theology of Reconciliation* (Wilton: Morehouse Barlow, 1984), 14-15. Hereafter cited as Hyde, *Toward a Pastoral Theology of Reconciliation...*

³⁴ K.B. Osborne, *Reconciliation and Justification: The Sacrament and its Theology* (New York: Paulist Press, 1990), 92. Hereafter cited as Osborne, *Reconciliation and Justification...*

³⁵ D. Solle, *Thinking about God: An Introduction to Theology*, translated by J. Bowden (London: SCM Press, 1990), 79. Hereafter cited as Solle, *An Introduction to Theology...*

[36] Solle, *An Introduction to Theology...99.*

[37] Soukup, "Theological Understandings of Reconciliation"... 26.

[38] Simon Sukumar, "Violence, Terrorism, and Reconciliation: Christian Theological Interpretation," in *Peace at Hand: A Hand Book of Biblical Studies and Essays,* edited by Paul Francis Ravichandran (Chennai: Church of South India, 2002), 205.

[39] Hyde, *Toward a Pastoral Theology of Reconciliation...17.*

[40] B. Poshmann, *Penance and the Anointing of the Sick* (New York: Herder and Herder, 1964), 3.

[41] William Telfer, *The Forgiveness of Sin* (Philadelphia: Muhlenberg Press, 1960), 19.

[42] Paul Althaus, *The Theology of Martin Luther*, Translated by Robert C. Schultz (Philadelphia: Fortress Press, 1966), 222. Hereafter cited as Paul Althaus, *The Theology of Martin Luther...*

[43] Paul Althaus, *The Theology of Martin Luther...201.*

[44] Wilhelm Niesel, *The Theology of Calvin*, translated by Harold Knight (Michigan: Baker Book House, 1956), 127.

[45] Hyde, *To Declare God's Forgiveness...19.*

[46] Hyde, *To Declare God's Forgiveness...197.*

[47] Grills between priest and penitent were set up and confessional boxes were invented. See Sean Wales, *Be Reconciled: Going to Confession Today* (Bangalore: Redemptorist Publications India, 1998), 21. Hereafter cited as Sean Wales, *Be Reconciled...*

[48] Sean Wales, *Be Reconciled...21.*

[49] K.B. Osborne, *Reconciliation and Justification: The Sacrament and its Theology* (New York: Paulist Press, 1990), 143. Hereafter cited as Osborne, *Reconciliation and Justification...*

[50] Solle, *Thinking about God: An Introduction to Theology...86.*

[51] Soukup, *"Theological Understanding of Reconciliation"...27.*

[52] Hyde, *To Declare God's Forgiveness...29-30.*

[53] Osborne, *Reconciliation and Justification...209-210.*

[54] Leonardo Boff, "The originality of the Theology of Liberation" in *Future of Liberation Theology: Essays in Honour of Gustavo Gutierrez*, edited by Marc Ellis and Otto Maduro (Maryknoll: Orbis Books, 1989), 42.

⁵⁵ Gustavo Gutierrez, *A Liberation Theology* (Maryknoll: Orbis Books, 1973), 36-37.

⁵⁶ O.V. Jathanna. "The Ministry of Reconciliation," *Masihi Sevak: Journal of Christian Ministry* XXVI/2 (July 2001):10. Hereafter cited as Jathanna, "The Ministry of Reconciliation,"...

Hemkham: A Theological Paradigm for Reconciliation in the Kuki Society

The assessment of the dilemmas of the Kuki in the first chapter indicates that their lives of conflict and fear make reconciliation the most urgent need for them. At the same time in second and third chapters respectively, attempt has been made to bring out the meaning, concept and practice of reconciliation, both from the Christian and traditional Kuki understanding of reconciliation. As the outcome, the current chapter proposes a contextual Christian theology of reconciliation - a Kuki perspective, taking into consideration both the Christian and Kuki traditional understanding of reconciliation based on *Hemkham*.

Issues in the Emergence of Contextual theology

The emergence of new ways of interpreting the gospel in response to contextual realities has been in currency. Liberation theology in the 1970's arose as a search for just society. The search for a just society developed out of the deep experiences of oppression, exploitation, and alienation.

In the same way, for Dalit theology, the gospel is good news about the liberation of Dalits from the oppressive caste system and social stigma.[1] On the same line, the women liberation movement also emerged and championed the liberation of women from traditional patriarchal practices and male domination. Thus, it is apparent that the contextualization of Christian theology or any other kind of theology is liberative in essence, because it emerged as a resistance to alien thoughts and ideas. A perusal of the nature of this theology exhibits that, it took the context seriously as the basis for developing theology while keeping the Christian truth intact. The trends today expose that social, political, historical, traditional and economic contexts have to be taken seriously in order to make Christian theology relevant for the people.

The Need of Contextualizing in the Kuki Society

Following the dawn of Christianity in 1910[2], minimal attempt has been made as far as theologizing is concerned in the Kuki society. Until recently, the Kuki Christian adhered strictly to theology promulgated by the Baptist and Welsh missionary more than a century ago. "To this day most of the tribal Christian holds that to be authentically Christian they must shun their cultures and embrace every norm espoused by the western church," says Vashum.[3] True to this statement, the kind of Christianity being practiced by the Kukis is still a legacy of the nineteenth century evangelical western Christianity which is alien to the local culture. Keitzar asserts that, the gospel message must be interpreted in the context of the people so that it may be really meaningful and relevant to the people. On this ground, revitalization of Christianity is needed if it is to be a people oriented Christianity. A tribal Christianity that is grounded on the historic faith of the Christian Church and an indigenous Christianity that is planted in the cultural life of the people side by side is needed more.[4] As such, for the gospel to be firmly rooted in the Kukis' ethos, Jesus has to be reincarnated, be born and nurtured as a Kuki. Only then, Jesus can become relevant to the Kuki. Presenting Jesus to the Kuki in this mode would be most befitting in their context. As a response, to make the gospel relevant and meaningful to the Kuki a serious consideration has to be given to their ground realities. In other words, contextualization becomes a necessity to interpret the Christian message relevantly to the kukis.

Beyond doubt, Christianity is an eye-opener for the Kuki as the missionaries were the first to open clinics, hospitals, education centres, and also to proclaim the good news of Jesus Christ. Reluctantly yet, it has to be admitted that the theology that is being adhered to by the Kuki Christian until today had come through the western cultural interpretation which overlooked the Kukis' cultures. Out of ignorance, for way too long, the Kukis have been conditioned to think that the form of Christianity that came to them through the first missionary was the only genuine Christianity. On this line, Keitzar rightly argues, the tribals forget the fact that the theological ideas that have come to them are reinterpretations of western people in the context of their cultural ideas wholesale, without appropriating the raw materials, into our religious practices.[5] In reversal therefore, the Kukis today need theologizing from the Kuki perspective, that is grounded both on the historic faith of the Christian Church and an indigenous Christianity that is planted deeply in the cultural life, so that, Christian message can penetrate more into the lives of the Kuki.

As revealed above, it is now more than a century that Christianity had come to the Kuki; however, theologizing from the Kuki perspective has been rather non-existent until recent past. Of late, few began to realize the urgency of the renewal of the Christian faith that came from the west, by incorporating the local resources for formulating theology that is connected to the soil and the people. From the Kuki standpoint, one such resource is to be found in the traditional practice of *Hemkham*. Seiminchon[6] agrees that, relationship and reconciliation between God and humans and between humans can be developed through *Hemkham*. Thus, *Hemkham* can be used to formulate a contextual theology of reconciliation.

A Comparative Study between Christian Concept of Reconciliation and Kuki Traditional Concept of Reconciliation

Notwithstanding some differences, the Christian reconciliation and the Kuki traditional practice of reconciliation have many things in common. Though the name 'Jesus' is not used, the reconciling dynamism at work in *Hemkham* is similar to the saving and reconciling work of Jesus. To the Kuki Christians, Jesus' teaching of reconciliation was similar if not identical to the reconciliation that is realized in the performance of *Hemkham*.[7] This may be one of the reasons why the Kuki spontaneously accepted the Christian teaching of reconciliation. On the ground of initiation, God is the prime mover in Christian reconciliation, while in the performance of *Hemkham; Haosa* initiates the reconciliation. Through the death of Christ, salvation is opened for humans, however, in *Hemkham* the idea of salvation is not at play. While Christ died for the whole creation, *Hemkham* is performed so that reconciliation between persons, tribes, villages, clans and families involved in killings can be attained.[8] In fact, one can observe that though they are not identical, there are similarities at a different range of degree.

Synthesizing *Hemkham* and Christian Reconciliation for formulating a Contextual Theology of Reconciliation

The Kukis have witnessed ethnic and factional killings, estrangement, and division and their tryst with these realities continue. As such, the need of the hour is acceptance, forgiveness and openheartedness. As divulged earlier, friendship, forgiveness, acceptance and reconciliation are fostered through the performance of *Hemkham*. Therefore, the spirit of *Hemkham* is indispensable if a strong relationship is to be established as Kukis and as children of God. Presently in the fragility of the world, the church is called to proclaim the message of peace and reconciliation. Therefore, every Christian has a role to play in this grand task of reconciliation which God offers. Salvation is possible only when one reconciles with one's enemies. It is true that the issue of salvation does not arise in *Hemkham;* nonetheless, the practice of *Hemkham* is an act of penance by the offering and the shedding of the blood of *Vohchal-tuhnga* which purifies the soil and the community including the sour relationship. Therefore, *Hemkham* is a means by which one enters cordial relationships in the society. The challenges and reality encountered by the Kukis prompt its Christian faith not to be confined only on spiritual sphere, and other-worldly salvation, but to be involved in confronting the problems devastating the society so that reconciliation can be disseminated to all and sundry. In the view of this fact, *Hemkham* can be a base, particularly for the Kukis, where any individual can participate in this pressing task of reconciliation.

Today a few Kuki theologians, realizing the urgency have ventured to retrieve the values embedded in the Kuki culture in order to make the Christian teaching more relevant to the Kukis' ground realities. For that reason, theological ideas relevant or meaningful to the local cultural background have to be taken and those not relevant have to be reinterpreted in order to make them relevant.[9] As such, the spirit of *Hemkham* which transcends enmity, hostility, and vengeance needs to be retrieved and acknowledged as similar to the Christians' reconciliation so that peace and reconciliation can be restored.

Jesus as Sacrificial Offering

Jesus as sacrificial offerings draws its significance from the Levitical provisions. In the Levitical regulations provisions are made for "sin offering" and "guilt offering". The sacrifice of a ram and the manipulation of its blood were necessary to regain the full health of community-life. It requires the ritual to smear or pour the blood of the victim offered for purification. "Sin-offerings" were occasional and related to particular offences of individuals, and different from the "High-Priest's" offering on the Day of Atonement which was annual and related to the accumulated guilt of the whole community. The prescribed 'sin-offering' was designed to include both the high priest himself and the people as a whole. The people refrained from work and humbled their spirit (fasting), while the priest was required to go into the most holy place where the Ark of the Covenant rested. This meant passing through the veil which separated the holy of holies from the rest of the temple and when he was inside, he performed a blood-ritual by sprinkling the covering of the ark. In this way atonement for himself and for his house and for all the assembly of Israel was obtained.[10]

In fact, sacrificial imagery is not much found in the New Testament writings. However, in harmony with the pattern and yet in certain respects in complete contradiction of "sins-offerings' of the Day of Atonement, Christ the High Priest of new order entered into heaven itself, once and for all, bearing his own life-blood to make an adequate reconciliation for the sins of the whole world and for peoples of all ages. The all inclusive act of purification has been made at the mid-point of the world's history.[11] In the epistle to the Hebrews we find striking statements as the following:

> For if the sprinkling of defiled persons with the blood of goats and bulls and with the ashes of a heifer sanctifies for the purification of the flesh, how much more shall the blood of Christ, who through the eternal Spirit offered himself without blemish to God, purify your conscience from dead works to serve the living God (Hebrews 9:13-14).

In the light of these facts, the life-blood of Jesus and the shed blood of *Vohchal-tuhnga* are both the medium of purification and reconciliation though the implications vary. However, in the reconciling and purifying dimensions they fulfil the act of reconciliation and purification. In the case of *Hemkham*, the offering and killing of *Vohchal-tuhnga* is demanded so that the defiled ground, village and society due to the murder can be purified by the blood which oozes out from the flesh of the *Vohchal-tuhnga*.[12] The performance of *Hemkham* in its religious aspect connotes passing through the veil of enmity between the people involved in killing.

Jesus as Reconciler

The salvific work of Jesus Christ is often portrayed through the image of Jesus as reconciler. The death of Jesus Christ is the base on which Christian reconciliation is built. In the New Testament writings, the image of Jesus as the reconciler abounds. In fact, Paul attested the redeeming works of Jesus Christ in terms of God reconciling the world in and through the death and resurrection of Jesus Christ in his writings. Going further, Paul writes, "In Christ God was reconciling the world to himself..... (2 Corinth 5:19), and in the letter to the Ephesians Paul refers Jesus as our 'peace' in whom all division and hostility is broken down making us one (Ephesians 2:14). In Hebrew scripture, the work of reconciliation is shown in a ceremonial context. Sacrifices are offered to atone for and expiate the sins of the whole nation. On this line, Vashum says, "Reconciliation is primarily the restoration of the broken relationship between God and the world and the restoration of the relationships between and among human".[13]

Peacemaking and reconciliation is also understood in the sense of mending broken relationship in the Kuki context. In the traditional Kuki practice of *Hemkham*, to evade the used of sharp weapons indicates the evasion of retaliation so that the sour relationship can be amended and reconciliation could be achieved. The goal of *Hemkham* is then to create a condition of *shalom*, at all levels, both individual and corporate, between the two antagonistic persons, clans, villages and communities involved in the killing.

Jesus not only reconciles the world to God, but also exerts every effort to bring reconciliation between humankind. The words of his enemies, "This man received sinners and eat with them," though spoken malignantly, enshrine the ultimate truth of His life and work, and it is through this truth that his reconciling power is felt. Such incidents in the fact as his gracious reception of the woman who was a sinner (Lk 7:36-50), his uninhibited acceptance of the hospitality of Zacchaeus the tax collector (Lk 19:1010), his ready sharing of the meal in Levi's house with his former associates and friends (Mk 2:13-17) all indicate that Jesus' ministry was essentially one of reconciliation. He came forth in the name of God to proclaim peace to those who had been enemies, reconciliation to those who were alienated and estranged.[14]

By associating and identifying himself with women and tax collectors, he was breaking down the existing social norms and recreating a community that is characterized by respect, acceptance and interpersonal relationship.[15] On the same line, the end result of the performance of *Hemkham* is to evade retaliation from the victim's side and the continue assaults from the culprit's side so that reconciliation can be worked out to reaffirm good will and friendship.

Christ as *Hemkham*

By all counts, though reconciliation between God and humans and between fellow human is realized through God's grace and initiative, this does not in any way bar human beings from taking the responsibility of restoring peace and reconciliation. More than that, every Christian is called to build up a society where peace and reconciliation reign and conflict is kept in check. In the bid to translate this wish into a reality the traditional practice of *Hemkham* would be of tremendous help in building friendship cutting across diverging barriers, and in bringing solutions to the conflicts. The performance of *Hemkham* is the coming together of two conflicting groups for fellowship involving self-sacrifice, forgiveness and acceptance by forgetting the past and coming forward with a new vision. Besides, it entails the two groups to reaffirm their relationships which had been broken by the killing.[16]

The whole aspect of *Hemkham* can be understood in the light of a bridge, because *Hemkham* is nothing more than bridging the gap of barriers, misunderstanding, enmity and mistrust. *Hemkham* bridges and mediates between the people to restore equilibrium in the society envisioning a community of unique individuals living in steady love and unity. On this line, Jesus' life testifies that, indeed Christ fits the category of *Hemkham* because he is the synthesis of all mediations (Heb. 8:6; Jn. 10:9; I Tim. 2:5). 'Mediation' for Christians means, "bridging the infinite gap between the infinite and the finite, between the unconditional and the conditioned." This is done through the sacrificial work of Jesus Christ. It is the reunion where the mediator has a saving function.[17]

By wielding the practice of *Hemkham* as a metaphor to explicate the dimension of Jesus Christ, one can presume that Christ performs the role of *Hemkham* by the mediation he provides. He sets the example by fulfilling in himself the dynamism of mediation of the traditional Kuki practice of *Hemkham*. Thus, at all levels, it is observable that this mediation permits Christians to comprehend the fullness of the mediation of Jesus Christ.

In the same manner in which the death of Christ brings together into a new community (Gal. 3:27-28), the practice of *Hemkham* can be a source in developing a contextual theology of reconciliation, though, in Christian tradition Christ's death is once for all, and reconciliation made through *Hemkham* is binding as long as no further killing takes place.[18] One of the most significant things about *Hemkham* is that, once *Hemkham* is performed and reconciliation is restored, it continues across generations in the form of re-affirming the old peaceful relationship or renewal of goodwill and till date no report of the breach of the relationship or reconciliation made through *Hemkham* is heard.[19]

Practically, *Hemkham* had brought peace and reconciliation among the Kukis even before the dawn of Christianity, and still continue to serve today as a source of reconciliation in the Kuki society in the cases involving killing. In the age marked by the acceleration of divisions, mistrust, factional clashes, ethnic problems; the precariousness of life compels the people to crave for a community where there would be "neither Jew nor Greek, neither slave nor free, neither male nor female, where all are one in Christ" (Gal. 2:28). Therefore, by making use of the symbol of *Hemkham* as Christ i.e. sharing, acceptance, friendship, peace and reconciliation; moves can be made towards achieving a harmonious community. Whether it is in the sharing of the fellowship meal or the sharing of the Lord's Supper, or the practice of *Hemkham*, a common idea of sharing, solidarity, fellowship, unity, forgiveness, acceptance and reconciliation is the embedded motive. Thus, Christ as *Hemkham*, as understood by the Kuki, envisages achieving friendship, recognition, solidarity, peace and reconciliation against the present state of hopelessness spotted with killings, clashes and enmity.[20]

Ankong-sokhom (a fellowship of feast): A Model of Kuki Reconciliation

Jesus' life proved that he was a peacemaker par excellence and this was illustrated in his relationship with the people. He lived peace in his involvement with the poor, the downtrodden, and the outcast. By sharing a table and food with the marginalized and forsaken, Jesus demonstrated his message that in God's kingdom everyone is welcome irrespective of occupations, genders, or status.[21] Along this line of thought, J. Jeremias observes:

> In the east, even today, to invite a man to a meal is an honour. It was an offer of peace, trust, brotherhood (sic), and forgiveness: in short, sharing a table meant sharing life. In Judaism in particular, table-fellowship means fellowship before God, for the eating of a piece of broken bread by everyone who share in a meal brings out the fact that they all have a share in the blessing which the master of the house has spoken over the unbroken bread. Thus, Jesus' meals with the publicans and sinners, too, are not only events on a social level, not only an expression of his unusual humanity and social generosity and his sympathy with those

who were despised, but had an even deeper significance. The inclusion of sinners in the community of salvation, achieved in table-fellowship, is most meaningful expression of the message of the redeeming love of God.[22]

As exemplified by the *Ankong-sokhom* of *Hemkham* as well as Jesus' sharing meals with those of the least, *Ankong-sokhom* signifies acceptance and the spirit of sisterhood brotherhood between and among the people; it signifies cordiality, friendship and goodwill. Both the *Ankong-sokhom* of *Hemkham* and the stories of Jesus sharing food with the least of society offer strong and tangible images that will inform and enliven a Kuki indigenous understanding of Jesus. These are powerful images which can guide and strengthen Kukis as they seek to re-establish mutual respects among themselves and will also serve to encourage the people sense of self worth. *Ankong-sokhom* is meant to be a celebration of the positive relationship people share with one another. It is a demonstration of persons or people being at-one with one another.

The traditional *Ankong-sokhom* of *Hemkham* relays the significance of sharing meals with one another in this time when Kuki society is being torn by disagreement and factionalism, this time when the Kuki society suffers fratricidal violence and death. In Manipur today, a theology of reconciliation would mean interpreting the biblical concept of reconciliation through the prism of *Hemkham*.[23] It would mean following the examples of Jesus Christ in letter and spirit and learning to lead the life that is informed by the spirit of *Hemkham*. Jesus admonished his disciples to be doers of the word, rather than passive listeners. Jesus said, blessed are the peace makers, for they will be called children of God (Matt. 5:9), the thrust of Jesus' message is very clear: "Go and do likewise." Be the agent of peace. Peace and peace making is future oriented and very demanding.[24] The challenge in applying this admonition to the Kuki context is that, individually and collectively one must assume the role of *Hemkham* as it is a powerful agent of reconciliation in the society. In the Kuki Society, *Ankong-sokhom* takes place when all enmity, distrust and suspicion are shunned and both the contending parties agree. It only happens when the people accept each other and are willing to further that relationship by forgoing any enmity or rejection whatsoever associated with the killing.[25] *Ankong-sokhom* signifies the bond of love, oneness, friendship and forgiveness. It also manifests that the partakers of *Ankong-Sokhom* have decided to see through the rejection and enmity, the possible bond of friendship which this fellowship of feast would bring about.[26] In this regard, the message of *Hemkham* can be a viable paradigm to contextualize the Christian concept of reconciliation in the Kuki society.

Christianized *Hemkham* Addressing Conflict Situations in Manipur

In the first chapter, attempt has been made to bring to the fore the conflicts between Kuki and the British, between different armed outfits belonging to the Meiteis, Nagas, and between the different Kuki armed factional groups. Since recent past, the signing of the cease-fire pact between Kuki National Organization (KNO) and United Peoples' Front (UPF) and Government of India through the Government of Manipur has abated the protracted armed struggle between them. However, internecine killing between the factional groups and between the different communities in the Manipur remains to be curbed. As a result, the yearning for peace and reconciliation is so resonant amidst bandhs, cross-firings, bomb blasts, protests and economic blockades; and the wails and cries from the debris of factional killings, ethnic clashes and communal bigotry in Manipur are so heart-rending. Therefore, the reconciliation mediated by Jesus Christ needs to be put into effect. Jesus' greatest mission was to bring reconciliation between God and humans and between humans. The metaphor of reconciliation points to the cessation of enmity as well as to a state of goodwill and fellowship. Having depicted the act of new creation which takes place when a human is "in Christ", Paul writes:

> All this is from God, who through Christ reconciled us to himself, not counting their trespasses against them, and entrusting to us the message of reconciliation. So we are ambassadors for Christ, God making his appeal through us, because for our sake, he made him to sin who knew no sin, so that in him, we might become the righteousness of God (2 Cor. 5:18).[27]

Jathanna also says that, God's reconciliation with human has given human the ministry of reconciliation. God reconciles with human to let all humankind share in God's ministry of reconciliation.[28] Thus, the responsibility lies in striving toward restoring peace and reconciliation for which God has entrusted all and sundry.

A Theology of reconciliation in the Kuki context implies applying both the concepts of reconciliation found in the Christian teaching, and the spirit of *Hemkham* in order to address the unbridled bloodshed, violence, factional killings and communal bigotry in Manipur. Jesus Christ can no longer be understood as embedded in the Scripture alone. It has to be understood in the form of more than just retelling the story of Jesus.[29] Jesus has to be experienced as one who walks down the dusty-pothole filled streets of Manipur consoling the unfortunate victims of stray bullets, or people caught up in sudden cross-firings between the faceless factional groups, or one who is killed in ethnic flare-up and gory bomb blasts. Jesus has to be experienced as one who fights against human rights violation and among the nondescript peace activists, so that he is understood more realistically by the strife-torn and human rights depraved people of Manipur. Thus, envisioning a theology of reconciliation which is meaningful to the Kuki in particular, and the people of Manipur in general, is one of the great tasks needed right away. On this line, *Hemkham* as a theological paradigm is most appropriate to contextualize the reconciliation of Jesus Christ in the context of communal bigotry, fratricidal killing and perpetual struggle. Manipur has been impaired so is the Kuki society and everyone dreams of a day when the present scenario is gone like an obnoxious nightmare.

Hemkham within the Cognate Tribes of Kuki

For far too long, the Kukis have been paying the price for the enmity, disunity, division, conflict and killings in the society. With the issues, ranging from factional killings to killings on the line of tribes down to the clans, the society has been weakened so much so that they have become insecure and vulnerable. The insecurity consequently impinges upon their spiritual lives. In fact, each cognate tribes and factional armed groups hold their standpoint as if it has been the only truth. Indeed, they consolidate the enmity and misunderstandings by not trying to sort it out wholeheartedly. This mental set up on the part of the Kukis leaves no room for reconciliation and urgently requires the mediation spirit of *Hemkham*. In this context, the spirit of *Hemkham* with its reconciling dynamism has to be put into practice so that the cognate tribes and factional groups can see through the enmity the possibility of reconciliation. Though *Hemkham* has been practiced in the Kuki society across the ages, its spirit is yet to permeate the society.[30] The permeation of the spirit of Hemkham in the society would mean shunning violence, enmity and disunity which have shackled them for too long. Applying *Hemkham* in the Kuki context would mean saying 'enough to fratricidal killings" in words and deeds, and find a common ground based on the common cultures, tradition and history of all the cognate tribes and factional groups. They have to see through the enmity and misunderstanding the possibility of reconciliation through the inherited common past. Perhaps, for each possible reason of enmity there are more reasons for friendship, sharing, unity and fellowship as they inherited common cultures, tradition and history. Reconciliation through *Hemkham* in line with the reconciliation offered by Christ implies applying both the concepts of reconciliation found in the Christian teaching, and the spirit of *Hemkham* in order to address the unbridled bloodshed, violence, factional killings among the cognate tribes in the Kuki society. The motive behind reconciling the cognate Kuki tribes has to be sharing, unity and for a stronger Kuki society. At the same time, the reconciled Kuki society has to be envisioned in the light of a stronger reconciled Manipur where the Kuki, Naga, Meiteis and other communities live in harmony and mutual respect.[31] The reconciliation of the cognate Kuki tribes in any way is not to be projected towards attacking, subjugating and killing other communities of Manipur. On the other hand, the Kukis by reconciling themselves and by their reconciled lives should challenge the strife-torn people of Manipur to endeavour for reconciliation at all levels of life.

Hemkham between the Kuki and Other Communities

Practically, the immediate need in Manipur is the performance of *Hemkham* between the Kuki and the Naga so that they live as neighbor and no more as enemy. The impasse that has been experienced in Manipur for more than a hundred days[32] due to United Naga Council (UNC) orchestrated economic blockade is indirectly the outcome of the enmity between the Naga and Kuki.[33] In the Naga-Kuki ethnic clash more than a thousand was killed and many remains impaired, besides the destruction of properties and human rights violation. Even after more than a decade, no genuine attempt has been made by both sides for reconciliation for the fear of compromising their political interests. Claims and counter claims of ownership of land in some parts of Ukhrul district, Tamenglong district, Chandel district and the newly created districts of Kangpokpi and Tengnoupal[34] have crippled the relationship between the two communities. This is because in many places they live together and have their own version of land ownership.[35] Neither one of the two communities agree to budge an inch from their standpoint. And it is here that the maladies of

Manipur especially those of the hills lie. In this context, the reconciling acts of Christ and the reconciling dynamism of *Hemkham* have to be lived out by the two communities. Ironically, majority of both the Kukis and Nagas are Christians and they have failed miserably to live out their faith though their towns and villages are adorned with magnificent church buildings. As such, in line with Christ's admonition to his disciples to be the 'doer' the two communities should live out the Christianity they professed by reconciling themselves and thereby reconcile with other communities of Manipur. *Hemkham* can be performed only when the different communities develop an attitude of acceptance and forgiveness. Sharing the gifts of nature bestowed by God in fellowship, comradeship and in the common inheritance of tribal ethos of sharing, communitarian living and care for the others would be the way out to reconciliation.[36] So much harm has been incurred so many have perished, thus, the way out is reconciliation through *Hemkham* in cognizance of, and adherence to the reconciliation wrought out by Jesus' life, death and resurrection. Instead of wrestling for dominance and attempting to foil each other's privileges and seize livelihood by usurping each other's land, the spirit of *Hemkham* has to take over paving ways for acceptance, sharing and forgiveness for the good of all the communities.

In the light of the arguments tendered above, *Hemkham* and Christian reconciliation are similar at varying degree though not identical. In fact, *Hemkham* cannot wholly represent the reconciling works of Jesus. In a way, they are world apart. The "perfect once and for all reconciliation" wrought out by Jesus and the reconciliation achieved through *Hemkham* with the possible extraneous influence and biasness in no way can be identical. However, the presence of the reconciling dynamism in *Hemkham* cannot at the same time be overlooked. It is through the performance and practice of *Hemkham* that God has been reconciling the people involved in killing in the Kuki society. As mentioned earlier, the role of *Hemkham* in achieving reconciliation in the Kuki society even before the dawn of Christianity was remarkable. As such, *Hemkham* would be the best periscope through which Christian reconciliation has to be viewed if the reconciliation which comes through Christ is to be firmly rooted in the culture and ethos of the Kuki. Keeping this necessity at the forefront, a contextual theology of reconciliation based on *Hemkham* has been proposed from the Kuki perspective. In doing so, the two concepts are fused in order to realize the 'holistic' understandings of both the concepts of Christian's reconciliation and *Hemkham*.

Endnotes

[1] Arvind P. Nirmal, "Towards a Christian Dalit Theology" in *A Reader in Dalit Theology*, edited by Arvind P. Nirmal (Madras: Gurukul Lutheran Theological College and Research Institute, 1991), 58.

[2] Thongkhosei Haokip, *Ecumenism Among the Kukis of North East India...*68.

[3] Yangkahao Vashum, "Jesus Christ as the Ancestor and Elder Brother: Constructing a Relevant Indigenous/Tribal Christology of North East India," in *Journal of Tribal Studies* 13/2 (July-December 2008), 22.

[4] Renthy Keitzar, *In Search of Relevant Gospel Message: Introducing a Contextual Christian Theology for North east India* (Guwahati: Christian Literature Centre, 1995), 63. Hereafter cited as Renthy Keitzar, *In Search of Relevant Gospel Message...*

[5] Renthy Keitzar...*In Search of Relevant Gospel Message*...17.

[6] Interview with Seiminchon Chongloi, Dean of Academic Affairs, Master's College of Theology, Vishakhapatnam, 15 February 2017. Hereafter cited as Interview with Seiminchon Chongloi...

[7] Interview with Letkholun Haokip, Dean of Academic Affairs, Academy of Integrated Christian Studies, Aizawl, 17 February 2017. Hereafter cited as Interview with Letkholun Haokip...

[8] Interview with Paolen Haokip, D.Th. Candidate ATC Aizawl, 11 November 2016. Hereafter cited as Interview with Paolen Haokip...

[9] Renthy Keitzar, *In Search of Relevant Gospel Message*...17-18.

[10] F.W. Dillistone, *The Christian Understanding of Atonement* (London: SCM Press Ltd., 1984), 129-131. Hereafter cited as Dillistone, *The Christian Understanding of Atonement*...

[11] Dillistone, *The Christian Understanding of Atonement*...140-141.

[12] Interview with Seiminchon Chongloi...

[13] Yangkhao Vashum, "Pukreila and Aksu: Tribal Theology of Peace Making," *Journal of Tribal Studies*, XVI/1 (January-June 2010): 6-7. Hereafter cited as Vashum, *Journal of Tribal Studies*...

[14] Dillistone, *The Christian Understanding of Atonement*...270-271.

[15] Vashum, *Journal of Tribal Studies*...8.

[16] Interview with Seiminchon Chongloi...

[17] Paul Tillich, *Systematic Theology*, vol. II (London: James Nisbet and Company Ltd., 1957), 108.

[18] Interview with Jamchon Baite...

[19] Interview with Thangkhojang Baite...

[20] Interview with Paolen Haokip...

[21] Vashum, *Journal of Tribal Studies*...9.

[22] J. Jeremias, *New Testament Theology: The Proclamation of Jesus* (New York: Scribers's, 1971), 115-116.

[23] Interview with Letkholun Haokip...

[24] Vashum, *Journal of Tribal Studies*...8.

[25] Interview with Hemkhothang Baite...

[26] Interview with Paolen Haokip...

[27] Link, "Reconciliation," ....168.

[28] Jathanna, "The Ministry of Reconciliation,"...10.

[29] Interview with Letkholun Haokip....

[30] Interview with Letkholun Haokip....

[31] Interview with Shangnaochung Chithung, D.Th. Candidate ATC Aizawl, 18 February 2017. Hereafter cited as Interview with Chithung....

[32] The economic blockade imposed by UNC kick started from 31 November 2016.

[33] Interview with Hemkhothang Baite....

[34] The two districts were inaugurated on 12 December 2017 and 13 December 2017 respectively.

[35] Interview with Hemkhothang Baite....

[36] Interview with Chithung....

Conclusion

The world at large and the Kuki society in particular, continue to be ravaged by enmity, killings and estrangement, and it has come to stay unless prompt and visionary action is taken. Living incessantly in the shadow of sabre-rattlings, wars, rumours of wars and ethnic clashes; the yearning for reconciliation has emanated from the United Nations Organization down to the smallest village unit politically, and from the World Council of Churches to the local churches in the religious' sphere.

It goes without saying that many innocent Kukis have perished in inter- factional conflicts, and in their clash with other communities. The forces of callousness as a result drive them toward narrow-mindedness which makes them susceptible to suspicion, mistrust, insecurity and violence.[1] Therefore, an audacious assertion for peace and reconciliation is gaining momentum in the lives of the Kukis. In fact, the various organizations ranging from *Kuki Inpi* to the smallest village and congregational units are determined to strive for peace and reconciliation. Thus, the commitment to shun bitterness, division, pain and wounds inflicted physically or mentally either in the past or presently is becoming more consolidated. The longing to move towards reconciliation for the cause of liberation of the people from the bondage of hatred and enmity is in the air.

Indeed, the message of Jesus Christ came to the Kuki in the early twentieth century through the benevolent efforts of the Arthington and American Baptist missionaries. The gospel reached them in the form of education, clinics and hospitals; and the dawn of Christianity transformed their lives and exposed them to the outside world. In fact, the coming of missionaries was epochal in the history of the Kuki. With their coming, a new civilization was brought to them through their benevolent and untiring works. Undeniably, the works of the early missionaries were redeeming. However, despite their good intention, it is regretful that, the unintended demeanour of the missionaries was both the subtle and open restrictions they imposed on the converts' participation in traditional dances, traditional singing and other indigenous events associated with the tribal life. This onslaught destabilized the priceless values of local culture and resulted in the spurn of indigenous culture by the younger generations and the consequent cultural-shock and identity crisis. With the erosion of community spirit, individualism came to the forefront and the penchant for western ideas and culture took over the indigenous traditions, worldviews and ideas. In fact, it is observable that the missionaries were short sighted to see the serious consequences the imposition of culture would have on the social and moral lives of the Kuki in the years to come.[2]

It is vital to note that confessing Christ in a particular cultural context cannot be universalized for it is shaped by a particular people in a given culture. There is no final theology, nor is there a universal theology; for theology has a built-in obsolescence determined by its peculiar scandal of particularity. It is carried out by a particular theologian who belongs temporally here rather than there, of this time rather than of another period.[3] Therefore, confessing Christ in different cultural contexts certainly requires different theologies. In this regard, Thanzauva says, the title "saviour" though comprehensible and acceptable to all Christians, the term does not sufficiently express what Christ has done for the poor. To them "liberation" is of upmost importance, as such, they understood Jesus best as the liberator of the oppressed people.[4] On this line of thought, the conflict torn Kuki society needs and will understands Jesus best as the reconciler.

Apprehending the urgency to retrieve the traditional and cultural values, a few of the Kuki theologians begin to use the local resources in developing contextual theologies, which are more relevant and meaningful to the people. Of late, it has been realized that the Christianity brought by the missionaries in the early twentieth century hasn't fully penetrated yet in Kukis' soil and culture. Therefore, the task today remains to make the gospel relevant and meaningful to the Kuki people's lives, cultures and ethos.

Given the conflict situation of the Kuki, and a serious consideration of the need of contextualizing the gospel message, a contextual theology of reconciliation has been proposed based on both the Christian and Kuki traditional practice of reconciliation. This venture drives home the fact that the search for an appropriate theology of reconciliation necessitates the possession of an attitude of acceptance, recognition, goodwill, self sacrifice and solidarity.[5] The attitudes which come along with this realization include the willingness to equal sharing between every individual, tribe, community, and between the various armed factions. Such qualities can come only when the people are convinced that conflict, enmity and killings are not the solution to the current deadlock but the rediscovery and re-appropriation of the practice of *Hemkham* and live by the reconciliatory dynamism inherent in *Hemkham*. On this line, the cognate tribes of the Kuki have to be reconciled in the spirit of *Hemkham*, and the reconciled Kuki society should not be projected to fight against the Nagas, Meiteis and other communities in the state and beyond. On the other hand, their reconciled lives and rejuvenated society should be a beacon to other communities to strive towards reconciliation. The reconciled vibrant Kuki society has to work towards reconciling the people of Manipur in the mediating spirit of *Hemkham* and the reconciliation that comes through Christ the reconciler.

Therefore, by employing the practice of *Hemkham* as a metaphor for the reconciling dimension of Jesus Christ, in other words to make the inherent messages of the gospel more meaningful and context savvy, a model of *Ankong-Sokhom* (fellowship of feast) has been introduced in the light of the cultures, socio-economic, and political issues overwhelming the Kuki society. This model is proposed in order to pave a way for establishing a community of *shalom* which is more accepting and more accommodating at all levels such as, family, village and inter-community's realm. Undoubtedly, one can affirm that Christ performs the role of *Hemkham* by the mediation he lived out.

Given the fact, Jesus sets the example by fulfilling in himself the act of mediation of the Kuki practice of *Hemkham,* there is no ground on which the Christian reconciliation and *Hemkham* could be polarized.[6] At all levels, it has to be agreed upon that the mediation of *Hemkham* permits Kuki Christians to comprehend the fullness of the mediation of Jesus Christ. Thus, Christ as *Hemkham,* as understood by the Kukis, poses a challenge toward achieving friendship, recognition, solidarity, peace and reconciliation against the present quagmire of despair, killings, suspicion and mistrust that deter the Kuki society to realize a holistic view of life and the "reign of God' on earth, here and now. And it is here that the church is called to take *Hemkham* under its ambit and venture in the reconciling enterprise through words and deeds.

And in the scheme to make *Hemkham* relevant to the realities of the Kukis, it has to be transposed to include all the conflicts and not be confined to dealing with killings exclusively. In employing *Hemkham* to address the plights of the Kukis, it has to be taken in its theological and reconciling significance and not in its traditional understanding and literal sense of the term. The synthesized *Hemkham* with its Christian's vibe and reconciling dynamism has to move out from its nascent form of confining to killings exclusively. The parameter of the concept and understanding of *Hemkham* needs to be expanded to incorporate the entire gamut of conflict in the society under its ambit. As such, the theological and reconciling vitality of *Hemkham* has to take precedence over its traditional concept and limitation so that it can address any form of conflict and enmity.

In doing so, the possibility of *Hemkham* to deal with other aspects of conflict can be worked out. In the contemporary world, despite the advancement made in science and technology, the injustice meted out to women, and the destruction of nature out of greed remains uncurbed. In this regard, a research on *Hemkham* can be pursued to incorporate these issues as well. However, for the present it has to be regretfully admitted that despite the viability of incorporating women issues and ecological issues under the ambit of *Hemkham*, the lack of thought development and sources deter it. Nonetheless, the use of the findings of the present study will give a new insight making it possible to pursue a more comprehensive and accommodative research on *Hemkham*.

Endnotes

[1] Interview with Hemkhothang Baite....

[2] Interview with Letkholun Haokip....

[3] Desmund Tutu, "Towards a Relevant Theology," in *Confronting Life: Theology out of the Context*, edited by M.P. Joseph (New Delhi: ISPCK, 19950), 155.

[4] K.Thanzauva, *Transforming Theology: A Theological Basis for Social Transformation* (Bangalore: Asian Trading Corporation, 200), 154.

[5] Interview with Paolen Haokip....

[6] Interview with Seiminchon Chongloi....

Bibliography

Books

Banerjee, Anil Chandra. *An Outline History of the World.* Calcutta: A. Mukherjee & Co., Private Ltd., 1969.

Brief Notes on Kuki Nation. Imphal: Kuki Organization for Human Rights, 2013.

Dailey, Sydney D. *Peace is a Process: Swarthmore Lecture 1993.* London: Quaker Home Service and Woodbrooke College, 1993.

Dillistone, F.W. *The Christian Understanding of Atonement.* London: SCM Press Ltd., 1984.

Doungel, Lhunkhotong. *Chin-Kuki Bulpi Phunggui Thusim Leh Chondan Bu.* Imphal: Guite Doungel council, 1993.

Dunn, James D.G. *The Theology of Paul the Apostle.* Grand Rapids: William Eerdmans Publishing Company, 1998.

Gangte, T. S. The *Kukis of Manipur.* New Delhi: Gyan Publishing House, 1993.

Garrett, James Leo. *Systematic Theology: Biblical Historical and Evangelical.* Vol.2.

Grand Rapids, Michigan: Eerdmans Publishing Company, 1995.

Grierson, G.A. *The Linguistic Survey of India*, Vol. III. Part III. Calcutta: Government Printing Press, 1904.

Gruchy, John W. De. *Reconciliation Restoring Justice.* Minneapolis: Fortress Press, 2002.

Gunton, Colin E. Ed. *The Theology of Reconciliation.* London: T &T Clark Ltd., 2003.

Gutierrez, Gustavo. *A Liberation Theology*. Maryknoll, NY: Orbis Books, 1973.

Haokip, M. Thongkhosei. *Ecumenism Among the Kukis of North East* India. Secunderabad: Published by the Author, 2016.

Haokip, P.S. *Zalengam: The Kuki Nation*. Zalengam: Kuki National Organisation, 2008.

Hyde. *To Declare God's Forgiveness: Toward a Pastoral Theology of Reconciliation*. Wilton: Morehouse Barlow, 1984.

Jeremias, J. *New Testament Theology: The Proclamation of Jesus*. New York: Scribers's, 1971.

Kabui, Gangumei. *History of Manipur: Pre-Colonial Period*. Vol.1. New Delhi: National Publishing House, 1991.

Keitzar, Renthy. *In Search of Relevant Gospel Message: Introducing a Contextual Christian Theology for North east India*. Guwahati: Christian Literature Centre, 1995.

Kshetri, Rajendra. *District Councils in Manipur: Formation and Functioning*. New Delhi: Akansha Publishing House, 2006.

Lampe, G.W.H. *Reconciliation in Christ*. London: Longmans Green and Company, 1955.

Lunkim, T. *Kukigam Nam Kivaipohna leh Kuki Christian Houbung*. Imphal: Published by the Author, 2016.

Maitra, Kiranshankar. *The Noxious Web: Insurgency in the North-East*. New Delhi: Kanishka Publishers, 2002.

Martin, Ralph P. *Reconciliation: A Study of Paul's Theology*. Atlanta: John Knox Press, 1981.

Oommen, T.K. *Citizenship, Nationality and Ethnicity: Reconciling Competing Identities*. New Delhi: Polity Press, 1997.

Osborne, K.B. *Reconciliation and Justification: The Sacrament and its Theology* New York: Paulist Press, 1990.

Poshmann, B. *Penance and the Anointing of the Sick*. New York: Herder and Herder, 1964.

Ray, Ashok Kumar. *Authority and Legitimacy: A Study of the Thadou-Kuki in Manipur*. New Delhi: Renaissance Publishing House, 1990.

Schreiter, Robert J. *The Ministry of Reconciliation*. Bangalore: Claretian Publication, 1998.

Shakespeare, L.W. *Guardians of the Northeast: The Assam Rifles 1835-2002*. Shillong: Directorate General of Assam Rifles, 2003.

Shaw, William. Notes *on the Thadou-Kukis*. Guwahati: Spectrum Publications, 1929.

Singh, Aheibam Koireng and Pryadarshini M. Gangte. *Understanding Kuki since Primordial Times: Essays by Late Dr. T.S. Gangte*. New Delhi: Maxford Publications, 2010.

Taylor, Vincent. *Forgiveness and Reconciliation: A Study in New Testament Theology*. New York: Macmillan and Company Ltd., 1941.

Telfer, William. *The Forgiveness of Sin*. Philadelphia: Muhlenberg Press, 1960.

Thanzauva, K. *Transforming Theology: A Theological Basis for Theological Transformation*. Bangalore: Asia Trading Corporation, 2002.

Tillich, Paul. *Systematic Theology*. Vol. II. London: James Nisbet and Company Ltd., 1957.

Traditional Policy and Political Stand Point of Kuki Inpi. Imphal: Kuki Inpi Manipur, 1995.

Wales, Sean. *Be Reconciled: Going to Confession Today*. Bangalore: Redemptorist Publications India, 1998.

Works of Martin Luther. Vol.1. Philadelphia: Muhlenberg Press, 1915.

Edited Books

Boff, Leonardo. "The originality of the Theology of Liberation." In *Future of Liberation Theology: Essays in Honour of Gustavo Gutierrez*. Edited by Marc Ellis and Otto Maduro. Maryknoll, NY: Orbis Books, 1989.

Chongloi, Satkhokai. "Conflict resolution in North East India: Perspective from the Kuki Christians." In *Peacemaking in the North East India: Social and Theological Exploration*. Edited by Yangkahao Vashum and Woba James. Jorhat: Tribal Study Centre, 2012.

Chongloi, Satkhokai. "The Unseen Christ among the Kuki people." In *Garnering Tribal Resources For Doing Tribal Christian Theology*. Edited by Razouselie Lasetso. Jorhat: ETC Programme Coordination, 2008.

Dena, Lal. "The Kuki-Naga Conflict: Juxtaposed in the Colonial Context." In *Dynamics of Identity and Intergroup Relations in Northeast India*. Edited by Kailash S. Agarwal. Shimla: Indian Institute of Advanced Studies, 1999.

Gutierrez, Gustavo. "Freedom and Salvation." In *Liberation and Change: The Death and Resurrection of the American Dream*. Edited by Ronald H. Stone. Atlanta: John Knox Press, 1977.

Haokip, Rebecca C. "The Kuki-Paite Conflict in the Churachandpur District of Manipur." In *Conflict Mapping and Peace Process in Northeast India*. Edited by Lazar Jeyaseelan. Guwahati: North Eastern Research Centre, 2008.

Haokip, Seikhogin. "Genesis of Kuki Autonomy Movement in Northeast India." In *The Kukis of the Northeast India: Politics and Culture*. Edited by Thongkholal Haokip. Delhi: BOOKWELL, 2013.

Haokip, Sonthang. "The Erstwhile Territorial Domain of the Kukis." In Kuki *Society: Past Present Future*. Edited by Ngamkhohao Haokip and Michael Lunminthang. New Delhi: Maxford Books, 2011.

Jathanna, O.V. "The Ministry of Reconciliation." In *Masihi Sevak*. Edited by Evangeline Anderson Rajkumar. Bangalore: United Theological College, 2001.

Kabui, Gangumei. "Genesis of the Ethnoses of Manipur." in *Manipur, Past and Present: The Ordeals and Heritage of Civilisation*. Vol. 3. Edited by Naorem Sanajaoba. New Delhi: Mittal Publication, 1998.

Kipgen, M. "Initiative for Peace and Reconciliation from the Perspective of the Thadou Kukis of Manipur." In *Garnering Tribal Resources for Doing Tribal Christian Theology*. Edited by Razouselie Lasetso. Jorhat: ETC Programme Coordination, 2008.

Kipgen, Nehkholun. "Why not Kukiland for Kukis." In *Ahsijolneng*. Edited by Jamkhohao Touthang. Shillong: KSO Shillong, 2007.

Nirmal, Arvind P. "Towards a Christian Dalit Theology." In A *Reader in Dalit Theology*. Edited by Arvind P. Nirmal. Madras: Gurukul Lutheran Theological College and Research Institute, 1991.

Nogaard-Hojen, Peder. "Baptism and the Foundation of Communion." In *Baptism and Unity of the Church*. Edited by Michael Root and Risto Saarinen. Grand Rapids, Michigan: WCC Publications, 1998.

Sanajaoba, Naorem. "The Genesis of Insurgency." In *Manipur: Past and Present*. Vol.1. Edited by Naorem Sanajaoba. Delhi: Mittal Publications, 1988.

Sebastian, J. Jayakiran. "Baptisma unum in Sancta ecclesia." In *A Theological Appraisal of the Baptismal Controversy in the Work and Writing of Cyprian of Carthage*. Verlagander Lottbeck: Peter Jensen, 1997.

Sukumar, Simon. "Violence, Terrorism, and Reconciliation: Christian Theological Interpretation." In *Peace at Hand: A Hand Book of Biblical Studies and Essays. Edited* by Paul Francis Ravichandran. Chennai: Church of South India, 2002.

Thangkhangin. "Prism of the Zo People." In *Souvenir of 60th Zomi Namni*.

Celebration. Edited by Thangkhangin. Lamka: Publication Board 60th Zomi Namni Celebration Committee, 2008.

Tikoo, Ratna. "Ethnic Issue in North-east India: An Overview in Manipur." In *Political Dynamics of North-east India*. Edited by Girin Phukan. New Delhi: South Asian Publishers, 2000.

Tutu, Desmund. "Towards a Relevant Theology." In *Confronting Life: Theology out of the Context*. Edited by M.P. Joseph. New Delhi: ISPCK, 1995.

Translated Books

Althaus, Paul. *The Theology of Martin Luther*. Translated by Robert C. Schultz. Philadelphia: Fortress Press, 1966.

Niesel, Wilhelm. *The Theology of Calvin*. Translated by Harold Knight. Grand Rapids, Michigan: Baker Book House, 1956.

Solle, D. *Thinking about God: An Introduction to Theology*. Translated by J. Bowden. London: SCM Press, 1990.

Encyclopedias, Bible Commentary and Dictionaries

Bromiley, B.W. "Reconcile, Reconciliation." *The International Standard Bible Encyclopedia Q-R*. Edited by Geoffrey Bromiley et al. Vol. 4. (Michigan: William B. Eerdmans Publishing Company, 1988): 55-57.

Averbeck, Richard E. "Kpr." *New International Dictionary of Old Testament Theology and Exegesis*. Vol. 2. Edited by William AVan Gemeren et al. Cumbria: Paternoster Publishers, 2002. 689-710.

Lincoln, Andrew T. *Word Biblical Commentary, Ephesians*. Vol.42. Dallas: Word Books, Publisher, 1990.

Link, H.G. "Reconciliation." *The New International Dictionary of New Testament Theology*. Vol.3: Pri-Z. Edited by Colin Brown. Devon: Paternoster Press Ltd., 1978, 145-176.

Porter, S.E. "Reconciliation." *Dictionary of Paul and His Letters*. Edited by Gerald F. Hawthorns, Ralph P. Martin and Daniel G. Reid. Leicester: Intervarsity Press, 1993. 695-699, 724-725.

Sinton, V. M. "Reconciliation." *New Dictionary of Christian Ethics and Pastoral Theology*. Edited by David J.Atkinson & David H. Field. Leicester, England: Inter-Varsity Press, 1995, 724-725.

Articles in Journals

Cone, James H. "Theological Reflection on Reconciliation." *Christianity in Crisis*, 32/24 (22 January 1973):303-308.

Stulmuellerr, C. P. Carroll. "Reconciliation." *The Bible Today*. 79 (October 1975): 484-485.

Senn, Frank C. "Structures of Penance and the Ministry of Reconciliation." *The Lutheran Quarterly*, XXV/3 (August 1973): 268-278.

Haokip, T.T. "Kuki Armed Opposition Movement." *Eastern Quarterly* 6/ 1. (Spring and Monsoon 2010):16-27.

Jacques, Genevieve. "Communicating Reconciliation: The Churches Responsibilities in an Increasingly Secular Society." *Media Development* XLVII/4 (2000): 29-31.

Jathanna, O.V. "The Ministry of Reconciliation." *Masihi Sevak: Journal of Christian Ministry* XXVI/2 (July 2001): 5-13.

Jr., S. T. Kimbrough. "Reconciliation in the Old Testament." *Religion in Life* XLI (Spring 1973): 34- 47.

Longchar, A.Wati. "A Case Study of Naga-Kuki Ethnic Violence and Peace Initiative." *Journal of Tribal Studies: Tribal Ethics VI/ 2* (July-December 2001): 102-113.

Peter, Michael Hansell. "Why was the Shepherd of Hermas left out of the New Testament Canon? A Contextual Study in Church History and its Contemporary Relevance." *Bangalore Theological Forum* XXXIV/ 2 (December, 2002): 42-43.

Vashum, Yangkahao. "Pukreila and Aksu: Tribal Theology of Peace Making." *Journal of Tribal Studies*, XVI/1 (January-June 2010): 1-15.

Vashum, Yangkahao. "Jesus Christ as the Ancestor and Elder Brother: Constructing a Relevant Indigenous/Tribal Christology of North East India." *Journal of Tribal Studies* 13/2 (July-December 2008): 21-36.

Soukup, Paul A. "Theological Understandings of Reconciliation." *Media Development* XLVII/4 (2000): 24-28.

Unpublished Thesis

Haokip, T. Tongkholun. "The Kuki National Assembly: The Party's Role in the State Politics of Manipur." M. Phil. dissertation, NEHU, 1993.

Memoranda and Press Release

Press Release of the Kuki Students' Organization, Delhi (KSO-D), 23 March, 2007, New Delhi.

"Final Peace Accord between Zomis and Kukis for Restoration of Peace and Normalcy." Signed on 1 October, 1998 at Churachandpur.

Memorandum of Kuki Movement for Human Rights. Addressed to the Prime Minister of India, 13 August, 2004.

Newspapers and Magazines

The North-East Sun XII/23 (July 1-15, 2007):22-26.

Jansen, Michael. "The Terrorism Trap." *Sunday Herald*, 15 September 2002, 4.

Poknapham (Imphal) 28 October, 2016, 1.

The Imphal Free Press (Imphal), 13 January 2005, 1.

The Sangai Express (Imphal) 13 June, 2007.

The Sangai Express (Imphal) 28 October, 2016, 1.

The Thinglhang Post (Churachandpur), 5 April, 2005, 2.

Personal Interviews

Baite, Hemkhothang. Chief of Litan Sareikhong, Ukhrul District Manipur, 6 October 2016.

Baite, Jamchon. Village Secretary of B. Phaicham Churachandpur, 6 June 2016.

Baite, Nehlhun. Church Elder of T. Lailoiphai Presbyterian Church, 3 November 2016.

Baite, Thangkhojang. Chief of B. Phaicham, Churachandpur district Manipur, 28 September 2016.

Chithung, Shangnaochung. D.Th. Candidate ATC Aizawl. 18 February 2017.

Chongloi, Seiminchon. Dean of Academic affairs, Master's College of Theology, Vishakhapatnam, 15 February 2017.

Haokip, Letkholun. Dean of Academic Affairs, Academy of Integrated Christian Studies, Aizawl, 17 February 2017.

Haokip, Paolen. D.Th. Candidate ATC Aizawl, 11 November 2016.

Khongsai, Khuppao. Chief of Molnom Village Ukhrul District, 16 October 2016.

Lunkim, T. Administrative Secretary Kuki Christian Church, Imphal, 18 October 2016.

Mangte, Lhunthang. Khongsai Veng, One of the Participants in the performance of the *Hemkham*, 17 October, 2016.

www.ingramcontent.com/pod-product-compliance
Lightning Source LLC
Chambersburg PA
CBHW030527260626
47157CB00005B/1906